Being Kidnapped

Dorothy Geller

Contents

Chapter 1/ kidnapped?

A riel's POV

When I woke up today, it was unfourtunatly to the sound of my alarm, which sounded a little like, "WAKE YOUR ASS UP, ARIEL! WAKE YOUR ASS UP!"

I mean, what can you do? A little pissed, I got dressed in a cute yet simple outfit and did my hair and makeup. My outfit consisted of a simple red t-shirt, grey ripped jeans and black combat boots. A little sluggish, I went downstairs and greeted my parents.

"Good morning mom and dad." I said, trying to look cheerful.

"Good morning sweetheart." My mom replied.

"Good morning honey. It's your first day of senior year. Exciting am I right? My baby girl is all grown up." My dad says, wiping a fake tear.

"Dad, you're being over dramatic. I'm only seventeen. You're like fifty." I reply.

"Yeah, but you're all grown up. That's what's important." He says. "You're finally becoming an adult."

"Anyways... I'm running a bit late. Bye guys! Love you!" I say while grabbing my keys and stuffing my shoes on.

"Love you too, bye!" They shouted back.

I run to my car and head to Starbucks to get my morning Frappuccino for me and my two best friends, Veronica and Madeline. We've been best friends for ages, and we've been through the thick and thin.

After getting the three frappuccinos, I drove to my high school and parked my black Ferrari inthe parking lot. Entering the building, I spot Madeline and Veronica leaning against my locker, which was styled girly-ish and tomboy-ish. I am sort of half-half.

"'Sup girl," Veronica said, nodding her head as I handed her and Madeline their drinks.

"Oh you know, just enjoying my life. My favourite part is the part where my alarm clock rudly interrupts my slumber" I replied. "What about you guys?"

"That's interesting. We also happen to be enjoying our lives." They replied with a smirk.

Our conversation lasted longer than predicted, which landed us into being 'tardy', as our teacher Ms. Harris liked to say.

We entered our class tofind Ms. Harris in the middle of one of her lectures about the 'fascinating world of english literature'.

"Miss Ariel, Miss Veronica and Miss Madeline. Why are you three late to my class? You do realize this behavior is unacceptable, correct?"

"Well Miss Harris, you know what else is unacceptable? The fact that you're fifty-something and you're still single." I smirk. "I really think you should go shopping. It doesn't hurt to go to a mall. Oh wait, you don't even know what a mall is."

"That is no way to speak to your teacher, Ariel." She says in a posh tone. "If I must, I will send you to the office. And your university won't be very happy after seeing 'ignorant rude, and disruptive' on your letter."

"Gosh." I mumble, heading towards my seat with Veronica and Madeline trailing behind me. Ms. Harris continued on with her lecture.

"You guys want to come over and have a sleepover at mine tonight?" I whisper to Madeline, who was sitting to the right of me.

"Hell yeah." I heard Veronica whisper from behind me.

"Miss McKnight." Ms. Harris screeches. "Why are you speaking during my lesson?"

"Well," I start. "Why are you teaching during my conversation?"

"Out. All of you. Now. I will not tolerate such behavior. Get out." She says sternly.

"Gladly." I say, picking of my things and leaving the class.

The three of us decided to immediately leave the school and go back to my place to chill. Imean, its senior year. You gotta learn to relax.

It was toward nine pm when we started watching Netflix and putting the microwave popcorn along with the candy and chips to good use. Unhealthy things all the way! In the middle of our movie, three undeniably hot and sexy boys broke through the window. Newsflash: There's a front door. I get that you're breaking in and all, but did you really have to break the window? The last time I broke it, my parents made me pay the bill and it was a shit ton of money.

They came in and just took us. You would think they came here for food, but nope.

"What the hell?" I yell.

chapter 2 / are you serious??

A riel's p.ov

Recap: "What the hell??"

....

Ariel's POV

"What's wrong, princess?" The guy asked. He was the one who broke the window.

"Gee, I don't know. Maybe it's the fact that you're kidnapping us?" I deadpanned. "Oh, and by the way, that window is going to cost my parents a fortune."

"We'll pay for it. Don't worry." He said.

"I'm sure you will." I snort. I tried getting out of his grip but it was no use. I was just a girl that was just eating popcorn and candy and he was well, he was probably a lot stronger than me. His friends took out a bottle a dipped a cloth into the bottle. He took the three of the cloths and covered our faces with it.

I'm guessing there was chloroform in the bottle because the world soon started slipping away.

...

I woke up to a bright light shining in my eyes. Thank god it wasn't my alarm, although it's kind of worrying that it wasn't my alarm that woke me up. I opened up my eyes to see myself in a neatly decorated. Then everything that happened yesterday came into my mind. Damn it. I was sort of hoping it was a dream.

I think I should count myself lucky that I didn't get myself killed. I got up and decided to explore a little bit and try to get out of this place. But first, I needed to find Veronica and Madeline I opened up the door to find myself and a grand hallway. There were three other doors. I opened the door to find Madeline sitting on a bed.

"Oh my god Maddie are you okay?" I asked.

"Oh yeah. I'm doing great. You know, except for the part where we got kidnapped." She said sarcastically. "Oh my god I swear, this bed is so comfortable.

"Okay, yeah whatever but we need to find Veronica!" I said.

I opened the next door but I didn't find Veronica.

"She's not here Maddie," I said.

"She's not?" She asked, confused.

"No, Maddie, I'm lying." I deadpanned.

We ran down the stairs and ended up in a living room. There sat on the couches was Veronica with the three other guys. One of them had his arm around Roni

"What's going on?"

"Why are you talking to them?"

Maddie and I spoke simultaneously.

"Let's feed her to the sharks," Maddie said immediately after.

"Well, dinner's settled for the animals." I snickered.

"Calm down guys, I'll explain everything," Veronica said, waving out her hands.

"Don't talk to her like that." Snapped the guy with the arm around Roni.

I snort. "Yeah, and who are you?"

"I'm her mate." He answered.

"Her what?"

"Her mate."

"Yeah, um, that's not weird or anything."

"OH, MY GAWD," Maddie shouted as she started jumping up and down. "THEY'RE WEREWOLVES!"

"Maddie," I started shaking my head. "Werewolves don't exist."

"They do." One of the guys said.

"Man, fairy tales are the best," I said, placing my hands on my hips.

"It's not a fairytale princess. We're your mates. We wouldn't waste time on kidnapping a bunch of random girls. I'm Xander and I'm the alpha. I'm your mate, Jay is Madeline's mate as Parker is Veronica's. " He said.

A little shocked, I started backing up. I was about to make a run for it, but I tripped over one of the foot stools and fell down.

"Oh my god are you okay?" Xander asked, picking me up.

"Did you just say oh my god?" I snicker.

This is going to be a lot of fun..........

Hope you enjoyed the chapter my cookies !! 🖤🖤🖤

-Edited

chapter 3/that's cute

A riels p.o.v

Ariel's POV

After our chat, I went to the kitchen to grab some food. It's not my fault, I barely finished my popcorn from last night. A girl's got needs. After the explanation, they showed me my new room which had a bed just as comfortable as the other one.

House-

Honestly it was a castle not a friking mansion,and then there was a bunch of other luxurious rooms,then the kitchen and living rooms.

That's the bathroom in every room there is,crazy right?

After finishing up my 'snack', I went to Xander's room and saw the funniest thing ever. He was sleeping with a giant teddy bear, which was surprising because literally five minutes ago, we were talking. Deciding to have a little fun, I jumped on the teddy bear, waking him up.

"That's hilarious. I need to take a picture. Did someone say blackmail material?" I say, whipping out my phone.

"What?" He asks, mid-yawn.

"The giant teddy bear." I grin.

...

.....

chapter 4/ princess?

Ariel's POV

The six of us were invited to a ball. A ball. Our second day here and we get invited to a ball that was a few hours away. I walked into my closet and tried finding a dress suitable for a ball. But nope. There was nothing. I tried on multiple dresses, but none of them fit my style.

I ran downstairs to tell everyone about my situation. Everyone was sitting in the family room laughing and eating cookies.

"GUYS," I scream

I didn't think it was possible but everyone was able to jump up from their seats.

"Ariel," Veronica says, sighing. "We're going to get gray hairs before we're even twenty."

"Anyways," I say, ignoring her. "I have nothing to wear for the ball!"

"Loser, we're going to the mall," Xander replied.

"Did you just quote-"

"We're going to the mall!" He interrupts.

"Okay then..." Maddie mutters.

"Let's go." I nod.

...

We left the mansion and got into a limo.

"What are you guys? Like is your job to be rich?" I muttered that when I took in the limo.

We got to the mall and searched the shops for a good-looking dress. I was looking for a long lacy dress, Veronica was looking for a white one as Maddie wanted to keep her options open.

We ended up at Dresstastic, a store with the dumbest name ever. Their dresses weren't that bad. I went to the section where all the lacy dresses were and one of them caught my eyes. It was absolutely beautiful. The top part was delicately laced and the bottom part was elegant and simple.

"Dress, I choose you!" I yelled out. I honestly couldn't care if people heard me.

"Calm down, princess," Xander said. "I'll get it for you."

"Princess?" I asked, with a raised eyebrow.

"Yeah, I'm uncreative so I'm calling you that. princess" Xander said, with a 'duh' look.

I scoff. "Clearly."

Across the store, Veronica squealed. "I found, oh my god, I found it!"

"Show us!" Maddie and I said, running over to her.

Right next to her dress, Maddie found hers as well. We were all set. We checked them out and left the shop. We decided that while we were at it, we would get shoes and makeup. Of course, the boys complained about us taking forever.

"If we keep shopping, when we turn twenty-one, we'll literally be forever twenty-one" Parker complained.

"Can you shut up?" Veronica said.

"Only for you." He smirked.

"Please do." She answers, rolling her eyes.

I swear, these guys argue like a married couple.

"Can you carry me, I swear, walking in two-inch heels is hard, especially when you're carrying a bunch of bags," I whine.

A second later, I'm being carried by Xander.

"Massage me while you're at it, princess," Xander said.

"Hell no. You're back is like sweaty as hell. We're walking around a mall! How are you sweating?" I said.

After being carried to the car, I thanked him by planting a kiss on his cheek. His faced flushed and he started blushing bright red.

"HoLY! He's blushing! Guys take a picture!" I exclaimed.

"Shut up." He said, his blush instantly disappearing.

...

We went to a restaurant to get dinner and we were served by three different waitresses. Why three? No one knows.

"How can we help you? One of the blond chicks asked while rubbing her arm against Xander.

"Excuse me? Miss?" I asked.

"Yes?" She said, giving me a subtle glare.

"Did you just finish eating cake? You got a little something on your face," I said politely. "Oh wait, that's right, it's just the seven pounds of makeup."

"Table for six please," Veronica said.

The girl had the nerve to glare at Veronica.

"Listen, I would love to give you a nasty look but it seems like you already have one," Maddie said. Veronica and I smirked, while the boys looked like they were enjoying themselves.

"Shut up. You guys are rats. You couldn't get uglier." She said angrily.

"Too bad you can't photoshop your ugly personality." I snort.

And that's how we got rid of her.

...

....

How did u like the chapter am so sorry I haven't updated in so long like I've Ben studying in school and it was hard for me to keep up. I promise I'll update moreS

orry for the mistakes

chapter 5/ I forgive u

A riel's POV

After leaving the restaurant, we went back to the mansion. To be honest, the girls and I weren't really accustomed to all this. I missed my family so much and they were probably so worried. I think I should still count myself lucky since I wasn't in a terrible situation.

I went up to my room and started getting ready for the ball. I slipped into my dress and did my makeup and hair. When I finished getting ready, I went downstairs.

"You look gorgeous, princess," He said with a cute smile.

"Thanks," I smiled back.

...

We left the mansion in a limo. Maddie hooked her phone up with the aux cord and we started singing our hearts out. Unfortunately for us, the ride was pretty short and we were unable to finish our concert.

When we stepped out of the limousine, we were crowed by paparazzi. Th flashing was driving me nuts.

"Pose, hun," One of the paparazzi yelled.

Maddie and Roni immediately started to do their own catwalk down the 'runway' which was more or less just the purple carpet leading us to the entrance of the ball. I tried to look happy and posed a little, just for the photographers.

"Hey, you alright?" Xander asked, looking down at me. Gee, way to make a girl insecure about her height.

Just kidding don't eat me hehe.

"Oh yeah, I'm doing great," I exclaimed, a little too cheerful. Honestly, I could be doing a lot better. Like I said earlier, I was kind of missing my family. I mean, all I really needed was Maddie and Roni here with me but I miss my parents a lot.

"I can tell that you're lying," He said, rolling his eyes.

"I'm not," I said, not looking at him in the eye.

"Don't lie to me, Ariel." He said, gripping my forearm. I noticed how he didn' call me 'princess'.

"I already told you, I'm doing fine!" I said, shaking his grip off and throwing my hands up into the air.

He looked around, seeing if anyone was watching and pulled me through the main doors. He took me through the ball, which looked amazing if I do say so myself. It was as if he had been to this place multiple times. We went upstairs and he pulled me into a room.

"Tell me what's wrong," He fumed, gripping tightly onto my arm.

"You're hurting me," I grit out. "Let go of my damn arm."

His eyes widened as the realization dawned upon him that he was hurting his poor mare. Notice the sarcasm. He let go of my arm and stared at the red marks he had created.

"I-I'm sorry." He mumbled.

"Yeah, like sorry's going to fix everything." I snapped, rubbing my arm.

"We should get to the others," I said quietly.

For the rest of the evening, I stayed away from Xander. I enjoyed most of it, hanging around Jay, Maddie, Parker and Roni. In fact, in the other half of the ball, Xander was nowhere to be found.

At around ten, we left the mall to go 'home'. I went straight to my bedroom, took a shower, and got changed into my pyjamas.

There was a knock at the door. Xander walked in, looking sorry.

"Ari- princess, I"m sorry. I really suck at apologies but I just want to let you know that I'm sorry. I know you miss your parents, but I promise I'll make it up to you. Somehow." He said quietly.

I hope whatever he does help in some way.

...

The next morning, I woke up to the most unexpected thing ever.

"No way," I mutter. In front of me, were shopping bags, the size of a small planet from my favourite shops.

"You know," I started with a grin. "Money wasn't the way you were supposed to win me over but this is working."

"You don't like it?" He frowned.

"Yeah Xander," I said. "I freaking love it!"

With that, a grin instantly lit up his face.

"Which reminds me, go look outside your door."

I slowly got out a bed, a little annoyed that I even had to get up, but when I opened it, I realized that it was definitely worth it. I was greeted by my family.

"OH MY GOSH! Mom! Dad! Bro!" I screamed. Did I mention I had an older brother? No, I think that didn't come up. Well, surprise!

"Thank you so much, Xavi! I said, planting a kiss on his cheek.

"No problem princess, anything for you." He said with a smile.

...

Chapter 6\Awwh,sank youu

This chapter is dedicated to @lilacoy for commenting and voting on this story. Thanks ♥

....

Xander's POV

I'm so happy that I made Ariel happy. I think making her happy is all that matters to me. Seeing her in pain makes it painful for me.

I surprise her and her friends with their parents and now they're parents live in a house ten minutes away from here. Don't ask me how they agreed to this but I'm glad that they did. Being rich has its advantages, and that includes making Ariel happy, although giving her materialistic things may not be the best way to make her content. Now that Ariel's parents know about everything, I'm going to do everything in my power to make her safe.

Today, the boys and I decided that we would ask the girls to be our girl-friends. If you think this is all moving too fast, well guess what? I don't give a shit about what you think. I spent over 3000 dollars on her yesterday but she deserves much more.

Me and the guys were ready to leave, but Ariel came down the stairs to stop us.

"Where are you three going?" She asked.

"Somewhere, why?" I replied, looking at her.

"Because I have... requests. Go fetch me a Starbucks drink." She said, proud of her own joke.

"We're not your dogs," I said, giving her a dead look.

"Are you really not?" She laughed, heading back upstairs.

"I want three vanilla bean frapps." She called after me as she left.

...

We were whipped. We tried to blame it on the fact that they were our mates, but we couldn't. We went to the mall and got them so many clothes. We were spending thousands on the girls and I sure hoped that the appreciated it. After buying them more than enough clothes, we got decorations and food. We got six boxes of pizza and got the girls their drinks.

I called my mom and asked her to pick up the girls and take them somewhere so that we could set up the house. When we were almost done, I realized we were missing something very important.

Candy.

How could I have forgotten about that? I flew out of the house and drove to Target to get the candy. The cashier looked at me weirdly when she saw the amount that I bought. Halloween was nowhere near right now, so there was no need for the excessive amount.

"Hey," She said, twirling her hair aroung her finger and winking at me.

"Not interested, bitch," I said while she looked at me with a shocked face.

"You single?" She asked, clearly not getting the hint.

"No, so do your job and fuck off." I replied angrily. She rolled her eyes and bagged the candy and chips.

I arrived home, threw the candy on the and wiped my forehead and sighed in relief. The girls soon arrived and when they opened the door, their jaws dropped.

"So... we wanted to surprise you guys and so, we got you guys a bunch of things," Jay said, scratching his neck nervously.

(Items for Ariel^)

(Snacks)

"So, we all have questions for you," I said, as I came closer to Ariel, who was now crying along with Roni and Maddy.

"Will you make me the happiest man alive and be my girl?" I asked looking at her nervously.

"Hell yes!" She replied, kissing my cheek, still crying.

"You didn't have to get me anything to be honest," She said, smiling up at me and hugging me.

"I did, princess and you deserve so much more," I said and she giggled.

"Aw, sank you." She said. Did she just...?

"Wait, where's my Starbucks?" She said, letting go of me. I quietly thanked God that I didn't forget to buy her that since she would have killed me. I handed it to her and she immediately started drinking it.

We finished the night by watching a movie. We finished all the food and candy. I think this has got to be the best day ever. We went to bed after that and Ariel came to my room to lay by my side.

...

Hey guys! I hope you enjoyed this chapter. I'll be updating daily on this book since you guys requested it. I'll be updating my other books as well so stay tuned!

Editor(@anney_314)'s note: I wonder if a werewolf eating a hotdog is considered cannibalism (I know nothing about this werewolf stuff so writing this stuff is pretty confusing).

Chapter 7 \ Taccoss

Hey guys, I would really like it if some of you guys made a cover for this book. I'll be showing the covers you guys make and I'll make you guys help me choose one! Have fun :)

Ariel's POV

The guys surprised us yesterday and I was so happy with Xander. He makes me happy and sometimes mad and annoyed but even then, who cares?

I woke up this morning with Xander's arm around my waist. I tried to remember if something important was today. I think ever since I stopped going to school I stopped stressing a lot. Yesterday was Monday so today- wait. If yesterday was Monday, that means today it's... TACO TUESDAY, BITCHES!

I stumbled out of bed only to trip and fall back onto the bed because of Xander's arm. I removed his arm from me and got out of bed. I quietly opened and closed the door so I wouldn't wake Xander up. I got Veronica and Maddie and together, we crept down the stairs to make some tacos. We got all the ingredients prepared and we got to work.

"Do you think this is gonna work?" Veronica asked, eyebrows raised.

"Well, I mean if they don't like it, we can just have 'em." I replied and Maddie laughed.

...

I was more than proud when we ended up making 60 tacos. It should be enough. I think. We decided it was to time to wake up the boys. Maddie had the brilliant idea of screaming our heads off so that's exactly what we did.

They rushed down the stairs, all shirtless and looked at us. When they realized nothing was wrong, they each looked at each other, silently communicating with each other and simultaneously nodded their heads.

They advanced on us and just as we were about to hit a wall, we all bolted out the back door and into the forest. I almost tripped and fell on a branch. I caught myself and we continued to run into the forest. We realized that the fact that they were werewolves meant that they were a lot faster than us so we his behind a rock. Smart idea, I know.

We panted and peered over the rock. No one was in sight, so we were in the clear. Or so we thought. A pair of hands grabbed my shoulders and I yelped.

"Guys we're going to get kidnapped again" I yelled.

"Guys I love you I hope we see eachother in heaven," Roni shrieked.

"Yes, we die together, we fly together," Maddie screamed.

"Will you guys shut the fuck up? It's just us. Calm down," Jay said, making us turn around to see who was behind us.

"Y'all are weird," Parker said. Really? WE DIDN'T NOTICE.

"You guys are the weird ones. Did you seriously have to chase us into the forest just because we woke you up?" Roni said.

"That's what you get," Jay snorted.

"And you guys are telling us to calm down," I muttered. "Anyways, we were just trying to tell you guys that the tacos were ready. And they're probably cold now, thanks to you."

Xander grinned at me. We walked back into the house and sat to eat the tacos.

"Are they good?" Maddie asked.

"Hell yeah," All the three of them replied, stuffing their mouths.

"Damn it," I muttered. I was hoping I could have them to myself.

...

i hope y'all enjoyed it as much as i enjoyed writing it. don't forget to vote and comment hoeeesssss <3

Chapter 8\ Blood,Blood and death!

A riel's POV

The worst thing in the world is waking up next to your boyfriend and finding out that you just stained his white mattress. Of course, I could always tell him that I have some blood fetish or something. Or I could tell him that I preferred red mattresses over white ones. And then again, I could say I was colouring a colour book and ran out of red marker.

If you don't understand what I'm trying to say, basically, I got my period. The only upside of this is getting free chocolates and excuses for anything. Don't want to go out? Don't worry! At excuses.com, you'll find an abundant amount of lies to tell! One's including your dead grandmother and having a serious cramp from your period.

Embarrassed would have been an understatement for the state I was in. My silk sleeping gown at been covered in blood and his mattress was nowhere near the state it was from the night before.

"Xander!" I cried out, shaking his shoulders lightly.

"What's wrong?" He asked groggily, rubbing his eyes.

I hid my face from embarrassment with my hands before pointing under the blanket.

"Do you need... Things?" He asked me quietly after peering under the blanket. His face turned red after seeing the blood on the mattress.

I chuckled at his red cheeks.

"Are you okay? Come on, let's get dressed. Do you need me to buy tampons? Chocolate? Anything! Just tell me what you need because I can totally go out right now and get anything you need. You know what? Here I'll let you-" He rambled.

"It's fine Xander," I laughed at him. I got off the bed and went into the bathroom. I took a shower and got dressed before placing a pad. I hated using tampons. When I got out of the bathroom, there were a few maids in the room taking out the mattress and changing the sheets. I asked them where Xander went and they said he went 'out'

I didn't feel like going downstairs so I laid back down on the newly changed mattress.

...

I fell asleep. I didn't plan to, but I did. I woke up to someone shaking me. Xander was back, and he wasn't empty-handed.

"Ari, wake up," I heard Xander call out.

I opened my eyes to see Xander holding a tray that had breakfast. There was toast with butter, eggs, and three bagels.

"I freaking love you!" I shout, almost jumping on him.

"I know," He winked.

"You're eating that with me you know? I'm not going to look like a fatass by myself," I said, sticking my tongue out at him.

"Well, you're going to look even fatter after you see what else I got you," He smirked, grabbing two other shopping bags still holding a couple o thers.He emptied them out and my eyes widened at the sight. There was so much, it was overwhelming. There were chips, candy, cookies, whipped cream.

"There's... something else I got you that I have to show you." He said, his cheeks turning red. He ran out of the room and went to get something.

"Uh, Xander?" I called out.

When the door opened again, it was not Xander that was standing there. Instead, there was a giant teddy bear in the room.

"I got you this," He said, his voice muffled from holding the teddy bear up. I could almost hear his smile. "You can cuddle with it if your stomach hurts."

"Priorities first alright? Food always, always comes first." I laughed.

Xander and I finished our breakfast in his room.

"Okay, I think we just beat the world record for most amount of food eaten in the span of half an hour," I said, slumping down and leaning on the headboard. Time to put that giant bear to use.

I got up and walked towards Xander. He raised an eyebrow at me and I opened my arms as if wanting to give him a hug. He opened his too, accepting my hug but the minute I jumped onto the bear, his arms went flat against his sides.

You see children? That's the look people get on their face after they get rejected. I laughed at him but then got up to give him a hug.

After finishing up, we went downstairs to see Jay, Maddie, Roni and Parker watching a movie.

"What took you guys so long?" Maddie asked.

"Having some morning fun." Jay snorted, answering her question.

"Guys, I'm drained. Leave me alone." I mumbled, hugging Xander.

^^ [EDITOR: IF YOU GUYS GET MY JOKE, I LOVE YOU] ^^

Xander placed his hands on my waist and smiled down at me. He picked me up and placed me on the couch so we could watch the movie as well. I stretched my legs out and screamed.

"Blood, blood, and death!" I yelled out, closing my eyes and sticking my tongue out, mimicking a dead person. Everyone looked at me for a full minute before laughing.

"Press F to pay respects," Parker choked out, laughing.

...

Hope you enjoyed this chapter!! Sorry I haven't updated in a while. I was busy with school work :(it won't happen again!

I'll be updating daily now so stay tuned bychess

Love you guys!!

Chapter 9 / Nachos

Ariel's P.O.V

So right now, I'm sitting on my bed eating nachos and a bunch of snacks with the girls,while watching a movie, we were watching The Thor movie,the new one it's really funny that's why we're cracking up every 2 minutes.

"XANDER" I screamed I ran out of nachos I want moree but I'm too lazy,no I'm that type of girl who asks her boyfriend for a bunch of shit,

He then came running in the the room, thinking something happens or you know haha.

"Ooof you scared me I though something happend,you demon!!" He said fake hurt,yep that's why I love our relationship because its unique

"I just wanted nachos" I pouted

"Anything for my princess"he said pinching my cheeks and pecking my nose."By the way princess we were invited to a huge party made by my dad and the theme is royal so just letting you and the girls know it's only for alphas ,betas and 3rd in command" he said

He tells me this now?

"Uh ya mind telling us when is it" Veronica said"Tomorrow" he replied casually "FORGET THE NACHOS ACTUALLY BRING ME NACHOS PWEEEZE WE HAVE TO DECIDE ON WHAT TO WEAR!!" I said freaking out not missing the nacho part

He just chuckled

"Okayy I'll be back"he grinned He's so cuteeee

God damn you crazy No I'm notSure your not

Yes fellow people I have conversations with myself well with my brain to be exact.

"TIME TO FUND SOME PRINCESS LOOKING OUTFITS HOESSSS" Madeline squealed

That's her specialty

We entered my closet to find a dress for me it takes a while you know when your boyfriend has put you a huge walk in closet, sometimes I feel bad when he spoils me because like it makes me seem like I have no money and like I can't buy things on my own . But he thinks it's okay to spoil me.

"FOUND ONE" Madeline screamed

We can always count on her with important stuff like this she's actually good with shit like this.

That was my dress pretty right? I look like a real queen or princess whate ver.Yes with that crown

Then we went and looked for dresses for Madeline and Veronica

And we found some.

That's Madeline's dress

And that's Veronica's

We then just put the jewelry and and crowns on top

Xander and the boys soon came into my room with a bunch of nachos and dip with 6 boxes of pizza

"Sank you sank you sank youuuu" I said and jumped on Xander

"No problemo I" he winked We then all sat on the floor and started watching jumangi

I got up cause I was thirsty but god had other plans for me and while I was getting up I tripped.

Everyone turned to me and started laughing

"I'm o-okay" I say while my face is facing the side of the floor.

Xander then came and sat looking at me

"What are you doing" he asked

"Oh you know just giving the floor a hug" I said smiling sheepishly

He then chuckled and picked me up

" I wanna go get waterrrr, so put me downnn"I said

"Nope can't do princess we're gonna sleep" he said popping the P

" I want water first and then I still have to clean my room an-" he shut me up by kissing me.

"I should do that more often" he winked

What's up with him and blinking is there something in his beautiful eye

I then blushed , my face was so red

He took me downstairs and got me water then another trip upstairs to bed

"I don't wanna sleep" I whine "and plus I still have to clean my room"

"It's already cleaned, I had one of our helpers clean it" he replied grinning

"Mmmm" I yawn"Let's get you to sleep" he said tucking me in his bed and cuddling with me"Goodnight princessa " he mumbled kissing my forehead "Goodnight prince" I mumbled kissing his cheek

....

Click!Click!

I woke up to some clicking noise.

"What's happening " I groan opening my eyes, I realized I was sleeping on top of Xander with my arms around his waist and my head laying on his chest while his arms where around me

And soon I also realized we're being filmed by the idiots I do call my best friends

I still love em tho.

"Say cheese bitchhhh" Madeline said taking more photos and videos with Veronica,Parker and jay

God damn these goons

"Cutieeee wake up timmeee" I sing in Xander's ear

"Hmmm"

"Wake up" I say"Five minutes" he mumbles

"It's 3 pm" jay says

"Say what now!!! The ball is in 3 hours Xander get up get up! " I say getting of him and dragging him off his bed

Yes I literally dragged him and he fell of his bed

Funny right??No? Okay?

"Ugh what was that forrr" he said

"Nothing we have 3 hours!! Clean your bed and start getting dressed" I said panicking not about getting dressed I could do that in like 30 mins I have to eat then do my hair and nails.

"Ok ok gimme a kiss first" he said

"Ya not in front of us" Parker said "Shut up you do that too" Xander replies glaring at him

"Whateverrrrr" he replied

"Come hereee" he said and I bent down he was still on the floor I helped him up and he gave me a good nice good morning kiss

"Anyways we'll catch u later" I winked and dragged the girls with me

We went and brushed our teeth and hair and went in Madeline's room so she can do our hair

She finished ours and hers 1 hour later

Mine with a crown

And then Veronica's

And Madeline's

We soon did our nails mine was beige and so was the Madeline's and Veronica's.

We soon finished up and there was 30 mins while we were going down in our amazing dresses , the boys noticed us coming down and their eyes widened.

" wow you look absolutely stunning" Xander said grabbing me by my waist and pulling me towards him.

"You look handsome yourself" I playfully winked at him

"Merci merci " he tried saying thank you in French

"You look like a real princess" he whispered in my ear making me shiver.

Oh I know I do pretty boy

" I know right " I said kissing his cheek, he grabbed my hand

"But there's something missing " he said looking at me

"What's that" I said looking at him raising one brow

"This is what your missing" he said pulling out a box that's the size of my palm

He opened it to relieve necklaces and a ring

"Awhhhhh their so cuteee,but u should stop waiting your money on me" I said while he place the necklace around my neck and the ring on my finger

"You deserve more then that princess" he said kissing my forehead and I realized he was wearing a crown ring too but you know a long one

Ayeeeee

I then hugged him real tight.

"Were matching" he grinned and showed me his ring

"Ooh I see that" I laughed

"Enough with the lovey dovey love birds We have a party to runnn" Madeline said with enthusiasm.

"Can I get the hoooooooyaaaahhhh" I screamed

"HOYAAAAAHH" The girls screamed back

"Our girls are crazy" jay whispered to Xander and Parker

"That's what's good about em" Parker said"Hell yeah" Xander replied

"LETS GO SHOW THE PEOPLE WHAT WE GOTTTT" Veronica screamed

What's with us screaming??

"LETS GOOOO" Jay screamed back

....

Hope you liked the chapter y'all I made it long just for y'all to forgive me

Anywho leave a comment and vote

Question of the chapter: who do you ship more?

Cyaaaa keep tuned for the next update hoess

Chapter 10\ Sorry

Ariel's p.o.v

So I'm here,well were all here at the ball thing,but like were still In the limo about to get out.

"whos going out first?" Maddie asked

"We are,we have to open the doors for you guys duh" jay replied

"Mais merci beaucoup (why thank you so much)" I replied in French

They boys opened the door and we got out,okay so I though their was not gonna be a lot of people but I was wrong obviously.Ya girl a big stupid ass that thinks no ones gonna be here well obviously they are it's the friking Alpha king with me.

Cue the face palm.

There was like so many people I mean wolfs who can turn to people,mannn this shit confusing are you human or not.

"Shall I escort you miss" some random ass dude asks and winked with a smirk,doing so licking his lips.

Sick pervs nowadays.

"Why no you may not escort me bitch" I replied smilling sweetly at him like innocent child.

"Ooh feisty I like it" I looked at Xander to see him closing his eyes trying to control his temper when hes mad he can kill don't get on his bad side.

oops,he lost it

He grabbed the man by his collar

"YOU DARE DISRESPECT YOUR ALPHAS MATE AND YOUR SOON TO BE LUNA?? LET ME TELL YOU THIS SHES MINE SO IF I WERE YOU ID BACK OFF BEFORE U LEAVE WITH MISSING BONES" He shouted

The guy just rolled his eyes

Xander punched him in the jaw and threw him on the floor,got down and started punching him,then I actually heard cracks.

I don't want the guy to die.

"Xander,Xander,calm down its okay" I said touching his arm,yes let's be cliche and touch his arm and get a punch while we're at it why not.

"what do you mean its okay?Your mine,how would u feel if some girls did that to me you would be fine with it?" he said looking me in the eye,well most likely glaring at me.

"What?No of course not I just don't want you killing him,its not good to do that,why would you do that" I replied back kinda angry

"Really??Okay so if a girl is flirting with me,ur not gonna punch her??"He asked,why the frik is he pisses at me I'm not the one who almost killed the guy,I get it Hes over protective but he needs to calm down a bit.

"well I mean,ill be mad ,ya but if she doesn't touch you I wont just hit her
" I replied looking at him.

"You know what I don't give a shit"he shouted,why is he shouting at me

Tears brim my eyes and I'm confused to why he's being so mean to me.I
slapped him hard and ran.

I just wanted to enjoy the night with him.

I need to go after him,I went inside and looked everywhere but I could not
find him.

I saw him standing alone,thinking and looking frustrated.

I messed up bad,now I was crying and I ran to him and engulfed him in a
hug.

"Xander I'm-I'm sorry can you please forgive me,an-and I know you might
hate me right now and I-I" I sobbed crying my heart out.

I mean who wouldn't?

He then hugged me tightly,and caressed my cheek,then smashed his lips to
mine.

He pulled back,and wiped away my tears

"Hey now babygirl we don't want your makeup getting ruined now do
we?" He chuckled

"You still didn't answer me,I want to know if you forgive me or not" I asked

"I just kissed you,what do you think?" he replied raising his perfect eyebrow.

"For the last time princess,its okay,were gonna have arguments sometimes
but,thats why we need to stay strong and help eachother up,thats what

true couples have to do,they have to fight together and pull eachother up no matter what,and don't get mad,i kinda deserved a slap,well not that hard,because now my cheek burns." he said chuckling

"Ya about that I'm sorry"i said while kissing where I slapped him,he just grinned

"does it still burn" I asked worried

"It hurts a lot" he smirks holding his cheek.

I then started pecking his cheek everyhere,while standing on my tippy toes and him bending down a bit.

"Is that better?" I asked one again after kissing his cheek like 50 times

"one more" he said

I was about to kiss his cheek,but the out of nowhere he turned his head and I kissed his lips instead.

"Hey!!You tricked me!" I pouted

"oooh yes I did!"he said pinching my cheeks and cooing at me.

"I'm not a baby" I said still pouting

"yes,your my baby,my princess,my queen,my flower,my cupcake,my muffin and my sunshine!!"he exclaimed

"Come one lets go show everyone who rocks this ball" he said dragging me there but not before fixing my makeup,what??don't judge

Tell me would you go in there would mascara running down your face?Looking like a rat hooded creature.

Then we entered and the music started playing with everyone's eyes on us,were dancing like theres not tomorrow,his arms around my waist and mine around his neck.

The music ended while he put me down with his hand on my lower back and we kissed,in front of what 578 people.

But who cares.

....

Hey guys,i hope u enjoyed <333

lots of loveee<33

have fun cookies,stay tunned for more

-Zeinab bazzi <33

Chapter 11/Im an elephant from planet mars

A riel's p.o.v

"WHO LIVES IN A PINEAPPLE UNDER THE SEAAAA??? SPONGEBOB SQUARE PANTSSSS" I sang with the song of the show

You might be wondering what's going on right now..Well nothing interesting unless you think me singing and being watched by your boyfriends bestfriends and his whole gang and including your bestfriends.

Ya oh and me jumping on the couches ,yep my boyfriends should adore me after this

Oh did I say boyfriends? Oops I meant my boyfriend Xander,and you know I might have another boyfriend called fries we have this strong relationship.

He loves me and I love him.

Perfect right???

No? Okay..

"Princess?" Xander called out to me"Yes my dear prince?" I asked looking at him while grinning

"Your so cute cupcake" he replied pinching my cheeks

"No I'm not you know why?" I asked pouting"Why?""Cause I'm an elephant from planet mars" I whispered in his ear

Ya if someone heard me right now they would think I ate something that made me high as hell.

"Ya but your a cute elephant from planet mars" he said touching his nose with mine making me giggle.

"Ya and your an ugly alien from saturn" I squealed,ya I think it's the food that happend to me.

"Oh am I now?"

"Ya" I giggled"Well can I turn into a monster?" He asked" ya a big uglier one"

"Ya and guess what this ugly monster is gonna do?" He asked with his beaming smile that can get anyone to fall weak.

"What"I raised a brow looking at him"He's gonna eat you"he whispered in my ear and it sent a good shiver down me

He then started tickling me and I started laughing my ass off cause if your really ticklish like me I think you'd be surprised at how long you'd be laughing.

I kept laughing and giggling

"S-S-top" I said still laughing

" gimme a kiss and I'll stop"

"You wish!!" I said trying to find an escape

But he held me in place

" princess it's now or never" he said then continued with the tickling again

"Okay okay okay" I said and pressed my lips against his,moving them in sync, we pull back when we hear someone choking.

We turn around and I litterly forgot about the idiots standing among us, videotaping us

"Awhhhh y'all are so cuteeee my babies" Madeline squeals.

And I blush in embarrassment. Xander just chuckles and pulls me to him so now I'm facing him sitting on his lap.

"Your adorable when you blush,love" he said kissing my cheek

So ya right now it's 9:34 pm and it's raining so hard outside and there's thunder.

"Oh ya princes,I have something for you" he said picking me up,my legs wrapped around his torso and my hands around his neck and my head laying on his shoulder while he carried me upstairs.

Boom!!!Boom!!!

I junped and squealed at the loud noise.

"Baby baby it's ok it's only thunder" Xander days rubbing my back and we finally arrived to his room.

He put my gently on the bed and went to look for something in his drawer.

He then pulled out a pandora bag and came and sat next to me.

He pulled a box out and opened it,it had three pretty charm bracelets who look absolutely stunning.

"I got these for you today morning when you were asleep to show you what you mean to me,your reallly special to me in every kind of way even when your sarcastic or trying to be stupid, your beautiful,stunning,precious in every kind of way and I just want you to know that I love you so freaking much princess,with all my heart your my first and last, and my forever and always" he says placing the 3 bracelets on my hand

I looked at him and my eyes were full of tears,don't mind the emotions bitches,it's called happiness.

"I love you too,more then you know, and you'll always be my forever and always,my first and last and your the most handsome and hottest person I've ever seen in my entire life,and baby you didn't have to give me anything, I feel bad each time you buy me something" I said kissing his cheek and hugging him

" Get used to it princess I'm always gonna be spoiling you, and stick with that cause I'll never stop,you deserve the world and more, your the world to me and even the universe" he said coming closer to my face and meeting my lips, we moved our lips in sync only are breathing can be heard and the sound of our heartbeats.

We stop for air, yes I'm not saying oxygen because everyone says that now a days like please please and please just say air.

What if someone does not know what oxygen is tell me?

" I love you" he said placing his forehead on mine

" I love you too,pretty boy" I grinned,oh ya and my bracelets look like this.

" wanna go on a date with me tomorrow?" He asked

"Why of course, I would love too" I said trying to say that in a British accent.

"We're are we going?" I asked

" it's a surprise" he smiled

"If u say so then" I laughed and he just stared at me with a lot of love,lust and so much different emotions.

His eyes were piercing threw my green orbs and mine were piercing there his grey ones.

"Wanna get changed and sleep while cuddling?" I whispered

" ya" he whispered back

He then pulled me up from his bed and then I went in my room to change into some comfortable pjs

He was wearing red shorts and he was shirtless,damn boy those eight packs.oof and those arms.

"Like the view" he smirked

"Oh yes actually, do u like ur view " I winked and turned around

"Why of course ,u look adorable" he laughed

"Lets get u into bed now "he said and dropped me on the bed and put covers over me,he then got under as well and cuddled with me,me wrapping my arms around him and wrapping his arms around me with our legs tangled together.

"Good night, Xander" I mumbled"Good night,love" he said and kissed my forehead

"Love u" I mumbled " love u too" he chuckled

Chapter 12/ Special date 1

Ariel's I woke up with arms around my waist and my head laying on a chest, I looked and stared at my handsome man and smiled admiring his good looks.

"You know it's really creepy when u wake up and see someone smiling at u like that you know that?" Xander said with his morning voice,oof I'm dying too cuteeeeee!

My face turned a dark shade of red and I hit his chest and hid my face.

"Your adorable"he mumbled then fell back asleep.

Wtf?

"Oh shit" he shot up and let me tell u it scared me to the point I fell off the bed and rolled legit

"You okay"he said looking down on the floor while I held up my thumb in response.

"Here mi amore" he said picking me up.

Damn that accent though

"Thanks" he smirked"You weren't supposed to hear that"I laughed

"Come on were gonna be late!"

"For what" I asked "Our dateee ""Ooooh,were are we heading to""You'll find out,go pack some clothes that will last you for a week" he said pushing me inside my room and inside my closet

"I don't even have suitcases" I groaned " I figured" he replied and went out and came back with suitcases.

"Hurryyy,btw babe" he shouted from outside my room

"What" I shouted back"Can u put my clothes in too please I'm gonna run to target and buy snacks"

"Okay fine,just be back in 20"

"Okay"

"WHIPPEDDDDD" I heard Parker and jay shout

"I KNOW I AM BITCHES THAT GIRL IS MY MATE OF COURSE IM WHIPPED" Xander shouted

Why am I here again? Nah I'm kidding

I went inside my closet and picked out a bunch of outfits for a week and I did the same for Xander.

I then grabbed the last bag for the snacks and hygiene shit like hair brushes,tooth brushes,tooth paste,and hair gel for Xander,I got a blow dryer and towels.

Xander then came in and put all the snacks in the last bag.

"Did u put me deodorant?" He asked zipping the bag"Ya I put it in my bag because ur bag siding have space" I smiled

"Thanks princess" he kissed my cheek and picked up 2 suitcases but there was 1 left so I tried grabbing it.

"Don't touch it"he glared"Why?" I rolled my eyes" girls shouldn't do that,it's not good for ur back,men should be useful too" he grinned

"Okay then " I laughed and left the suitcase

He put them downstairs and I went down too

"Where y'all going?" Jay asked

"Date" Xander replied"With suitcases?" He asked" one week date trip" I said"Ayeeee whatcha gonna do" he winked

"Ariel come on ignore the idiot "Xander said grabbing my hand and pulling me into his lambo.

While he started the car and we were headed to the airport which would take 45 minute ride, I turned on the radio and feel my love by Glenn Travis started.

I started singing to it while faking I'm singing into a microphone and moving my body to the beat,yes all that while singing

Someone told meLove was onlyIn the moviesIt don't exist in real life these days nowBut you showed meIf I only just find the faith I need to believe

Anything is possibleIf you want it bad enoughKnow the sky, ain't too highTest your limitsYou can feel unstoppableIncredibleAlmost there, I can see I'm so ready

I was singing my heart out and then the music stopped.

"Hey no fair I was enjoying myself u know" I turned to look at Xander who had a smirk on his face

" you have a beautiful voice princess,but we're here" he laughed

" yasssss now lets go let's go, I wanna know we're we goinggggg" I said while he opened my door and grabbed my hand

He locked the car and headed inside, we then went in the back and there was his own freaking private jet, I should have expected it tho.

"Awhhh it's so prettyyyy" I grinned happily

While he looked at me with so much love,happiness,lust,amazement and so much more I couldn't describe.

"Come on lets go wait till u see the inside" he took me inside of the jet and let me tell u actually lemme show u.

And there was even a bedroom

It was so big honestly huge was its definition

He grabbed me by my waist and carried me to a seat.

" I have legs" I groaned He just smirked and started peppering my face with kisses and I'm sitting there pouting, he kissed my pouted lips and sat in front of me.

"Can u pleaseeeee tell me where we're going pretty pweeeeaaaase with a cherry on top" I said *cough* more like begged.

"We're-nope I'm not giving in but I was about to and that's why I should pay more attention I love u though" he replied almost giving in ughhh

I'm whipped he muttered thinking I did not hear him.

Well I guess I'm gonna have to wait.

" it's gonna be a while till we get there prolly like 12 hours" he replied that means when we arrived it will be 11 pm at night.

A flight attendant then came in with her tiny flight wear and her breasts that are popping up.

"Hey Xanderrr what can I get u" she said rubbing his arm while putting her breasts on full display.

Oh hell to the no no no

" hey I'm right hereee" I waved

" oh I didn't see u there" she said with disgust

"Well now you did and please do me a huge favour and take your hands off my man,because it won't look too good when I chop your arms off with my hidden secret knife now would it,and for the record you need less makeup and more suitable clothing , so now u could leave" I replied getting angry

" and who are you exactly to tell me what to do or wear,and no he's not yours he's mine he called me pretty once anyways who'd want a girl with barley any boobs"she smirked

As I was about to snap at this hoe,Xander beat me to it

"Listen here u dirty slut,this is my girl your talking to and I never called u pretty whoever told u that was lying cause you look like you got gang-banged by crayola.I love this girl ,sitting in front of me so now would you mind getting us our food cause right after this you ain't getting no job cause newsflash bitch I'm firing you,get the fuck out!" He growled using his alpha voice at the flight attendant who looked scared as hell and she scurried off to get our food.

"Dang boyyy I'm impressed you just roasted her fake ass,since you did that mommy is gonna be nice and give u a kiss" I said and went and gave him a nice passionate kiss. After that kiss he just grinned and zoned out.

"I love you" he said out of nowhere"I love you too I'm happy I'm your mate
"I smiled " me too princess,the moon goddess chose right, we're meant to
be" he winked while I just laughed.

The attendant then came over with the food and then we started digging
in.

It was honestly good but I know she's the one who did not do it,there's a
chef there.

I finished my food and decided to watch a movie Xander then joined me
sitting on the couch,we were watching X-men.

I yawned and cuddled up to Xander.

My eyes were getting droopy then I felt Xander picking me up and placing
me in the bedroom,he put the covers over me and cuddled up next to me.

I then drifted off into darkness dreaming about my amazing boyfriend and
about how lucky I am to have him as a mate.

....

Thanks for reading stay tuned for the next chapter.

Where do you think he's taking her??

Anyways have a good day cookies don't forget to vote and comment

Chapter 13/ special date 2

Ariel's p.o.v

I woke and saw no one beside be,Xander must have got up to eat or something we still had a 1 hour flight and we'd be there,I got dressed into an outfit I found in the closet,I wonder who's clothes those are for but I'm not even gonna ask.

Wait as a girlfriend and his mate it's ok to be suspicious dun dunnnn.

This was the outfit I found which I'm wearing

"Xander xanderrrrr,where are youuuu" I coo trying to find Xander

"Boo"someone says in my ear,I jump and swing my fist but the person caught them before it hit them.

"The hell you were about to hit me,crazy women!" Xander hissed with amusement in his eyes.

"That's what comes to my mind when I get scared,swing em like you can kill em" I say proudly with my head up

"Damn this chick is crazy" he muttered"Newsflash bitch this chick is yours" I shot

While he just chuckled

"Damn right she is" he laughed and I smiled

"So when are we arriving to this mysterious date place?" Just as I asked the pilot announced for us to put on our seatbelts and that we were landing

We both took a seat and put on our seatbelts

5 minutes later we landed

I unbuckled my seat and so did Xander,he enterwined our hands and led us off his private jet

I gasped when I saw were we arrived at.

"OUR DATE ROADRIP IS TO DISNEYWORLD??" I squealed in excitement,don't judge i like Minnie Mouse and her little boyfriend

"Ya,I mean you said you always wanted to come,so I thought you'd like it" he said scratching the back of his neck nervously

"I don't like it..." I said while his eyes widened

"I freaking love it" I squealed and jumped in his arms while he just grinned

"Glad you love it" he smiled and pecked my lips

I love the smile

" How long are we staying here" I smiled up at him

"1 week" he said casually and my eyes widened"That's so long""Ya but we staying 2 days in Disney,then we're gonna go to New York for 3days and then to Dubai for 2 days" he said

"You planned all this?" I asked

"Yup"he said popping the P

"I Love you" I said giving him my biggest smile showing my dimples

"Love you more"he whispered in my ear while spinning me around

"Lets start exploringgg"he said dragging me inside the beginning of Disneyworld

....

We went on so many rides and it was so much fun. We were sitting next to each other right now on the pirates and the Caribbean ride.Im dying.

We went off and decided to go eat

"That.was.so.much.funnn" I squealed like a kid who's high on candy.

"I know right,it was funny seeing you scream" Xander laughed while I glared,and he just pinched my cheeks

We ate some hotdogs and then went around the small shops

"Awhhhhh I want one" I whined looking at the Minnie Mouse and Mickey ears

"Here let's buy one" he said dragging me there

"Hey what can I give you" a guy who was there asked looking me up and down

Xander pushes me behind his back and told him to give him one Minnie Mouse ears and a Mickey Mouse ears

He turned around and placed the Minnie Mouse ears on my head and I placed the Mickey Mouse ones on his head

"You look cute" I grinned"And so do you" he grinned back grabbing my hand

Is it just me or am I getting cheesy?

I am and it's scarin me

....

"Princess were in dubai" Xander said picking me off

"I have a question"

"Yes?" He replied

"How the hell can u carry me I'm so freaking heavy how are you not dead yet"

"It's all muscles babe" he winked

"And not your not heavy,ur light" he said after

"Oh thanks I actually feel loved" I laughed

"Hurry up and get dressed we're going shopping" he squealed

Wtf just happend? Did he just squeal?

Yes dumbass he did u heard him

That's when I lost it

I started laughing like a maniac

He just looked down embarrassed

"Hey hey it's ok it's funny" I kissed his cheek

While he looked up and glared playfully

"Now get out of the room I have to get dressed" I laughed while trying to push him out of the room.

Ya keyword "trying" he wouldn't budge

"Would u mins if I stay"he smirked

"Yaaaaaaaa.....of course not get out pervert"

"Ugh fine" he muttered and got out

"I'm making Pancakes" he shouted from the kitchen we had in the hotel. A really luxurious hotel.

"Wear something fancy"

"Okay"I shouted from the room for the 10th time

I washed my face and brushed my teeth and did what u usually do when u wake up.

I went in my luggage and found an outfit

I put on some makeup

And I straightened my hair

I went out and smelled the fresh smell of pancakes.

Xander's shirtless back was facing me so I went behind him trying not to make a sound and wrapped my arms around his waist and laid my head on his bare back

"You smell good" I tell him

"Why thanks I always do" he said turning around and he covered his eyes

"What's wrong? Is there something in your eyes" I said trying to remove his hands

"No it's just that your so stunning,my eyes are burning" he said peeking threw his right hand

"Oh just go get changed buddy" I said patting his back laughing.

He went and got dressed while I was eating the amazing pancakes with some lemonade .

Xander came out dressed and let me tell u he looked fine!

He was wearing that and you can see his eight pack because of the shirt

"Lets go" he grabbed the keys to his Ferrari and dragged me outside and inside the car and to the mall.

...............::::...

Right now we're in the mall carrying so much bags that my hand can barley handle,that's why we borrowed a big cart and placed all the bags in there.

We got a bunch of matching outfits and a bunch of clothes for me and Xander I didn't want to buy myself clothes but like I got threatened by a certain someone and ya it scared me so I agreed.

He mostly helped me pick out nice outfits and let me tell you he has really good taste.

We finished shopping and went in the car.

"Now we going to a restaurant the most famous one here" he said throwing a glance in my direction and grabbed my hand and placed it on my thigh still holding the steering wheel with the other

We arrived at the restaurant and took a seat

"What do you want to eat?"

"Hmm..a ceaser salad,fries,sushi and ya that's it" I said

"I'll have the same too"he replied

We gave are orders to the waiter and we just talked about how much fun we had and how he's going to be taking me everywhere and spoiling me.

This dude sometimes smh.

Meh I still love him

The waiter came back with our orders and we silently began to eat and we both took pictures of each other and he took some of me on Snapchat and wrote stuff like

With my favourite girl

Look at my gorgeous princess

Glad this girl is my mate

While I just cooed at his cuteness

He actually is so famous he has more then 25 million followers on insta and when he found out I was his mate and he started taking pics of me and posting them I got so many as well almost higher then him that's how many.

I went from 1 million to ya I can't even count million

On his and my snap we have so much viewers and shit

....

We went back to the hotel and I packed the things and with the 100 of bags that we got full of cute accessories and bags and clothes and shit.

Tomorrow we'd head back home so right now we went in our pyjamas and cuddled to sleep

....

Heyyyy I hope you liked this chapter don't forget to vote bitches

And should I make the. Chapters long or short let me known please I'm the comments

Bye again hoesss

Eat a rainbow - me

Chapter 14/ IceCream

X anders p.o.v

"I want ice cream " "No""But I want ice creammmm""And I said no""OMG WHY CANT YOU JUST GET ME ICECREAM YOUR SO MEAN AND AND I WANNA KILL YOU LIKE HONESTLY" Ariel screams and sobs on the same time

Confused? Well lemme just tell you someone is on their period and it's going bad for them.

She cries and sobs"Hey,hey don't cry princess " I said grabbing her by the waist and placing her on my lap while she cries.She looks up at me and holds onto my neck"can we buy ice cream?"

"Ya lets go" I said grabbing her making her stand on her feet

"Do I stay in my pyjamas " she asked,her pyjamas were shorts and a tanktop that showed her stomache

"Oh hell no,I'm making u put my hoodie over your head" I said placing one of my hoodies over her,she looked adorable with her small pouting lips.

I couldn't help it and I smashed my lips to hers,one of my hands on the side of her cheek and the other around her waist we were kissing passionately while her hands flew to my hair and she was twirling my hair around her tiny fingers.

"I still want icecream" she mumbled against my lips,I pulled back and she put her shoes on.

She grabbed my hand like I little kid and pulled me to my Bugatti.

I swear she's so cute when she's on her period because she acts like a child.

That sounded wrong Xander shut up

We arrived at the icecream store and I got her favourite,cookies and cream while I got caramel fudge.

I enterwined our fingers while we ate our icecream.

She kept giggling and laughing at the funny things I said.

I love her so much I wouldn't trade this beauty for the world.

"Hey muffin,you have icecream next to your lips" I laughed

"Oh well why are u laughing help me take it off"she rolled her eyes

"If you say so" I shrugged and took The opportunity to lick the side of her lips

She looked at me and blushed so hard and put the hood on and covered her face with it while I just laughed.

....

3 days later....

Ariel's p.o.v

Ok so I came to the conclusion that I'm a physco when it comes to my period.my period is over that's good.

Right now the girls and the guys are sitting with me watching dead pool,that movie never gets old.

But there are some scenes that like you know...

Xander had his head laying on my lap and his legs on the couch,I was stuffing my face as well as his with popcorn and let me tell you that sight is hilarious.

I soon felt myself drift to sleep....

I felt someone carrying me upstairs and up to the room then I automatically shut down.

Xander's POV

I looked and stared at the beautiful girl laying on my bed,I mean our bed. She looks so mesmerizing,her eyes,hair and just everything about her.

I heard a knock at the door downstairs so I tucked her in and went to check it out.

I opened the door and was honestly so furious when I saw who it was.

"Ricky" I said through gritted teeth,

"My dear lovely brother" he smiled

....

Sorry this was short updating a longer one tomorrow hope you liked it

Question:did you think he had a brother what's your feeling about his brother?

Chapter 15/The brother and the plans

Ariel's p.o.v

I woke up an it was 12 am to the shouting downstairs so obviously you would check that out am I right?because that woke me up.

I went downstairs and saw A man who looked exactly like Xander talking to Well Xander himself and arguing about something.

"Xander" I mumbled tiredly reaching out behind him to grab his shirt.

He turned around and took me in his arms.

"Princess,why are you awake you need to go to sleep,go now I'll be up in a couple of minutes." He said

Ya he thinks I'll leave after HE woke me up. Nah uh uh,not happening.

"N-no I want you to come now,and w-ho is this" I yawned

"Well come on dear brother tell her who am I" mr look alike said,while Xander gritted his teeth and held me closer if that's even possible to your thinking.

"Brother?" I asked confused

"Some brother you are!You left us!You left me!"Xander shouted

"Baby,baby calm down" I said grabbing his face between my hands,his tensed shoulders then relaxed and his face softened.

"You must be his one and only mate,you looked like a whore"

Uh bitch.He did not just call me that.I was ABOUT to snap the guys neck but guess who beat me to it? My mom!! Nah I'm kidding it's Xander.Hehe Zandy

"WHAT DID YOU JUST CALL HER!!???" Xander boomed while I covered my ears,why you may ask? Because he's holding me and my ears hurt now.

"I was kidding she's a beauty,she's really special I see,but that's not what I'm here to tell you,I'm here to apologize and tell you how sorry I am,I did a huge mistake and I know you won't forgive me just yet but I wanna be a better big brother"

"No Ricky"

"Why not??" The guy which now I just learnt is called Ricky said

" You left,that was your choice and now your not coming back"

"I promise you,I swear just gimme a chance,I swear I changed we'll go back like the old times please Xander"

"I'll decided gimme a couple of minutes,princess you decide for me" he said dragging me to the living room.

"What do I do princess??What do I do?" He groaned.

"Well if your debating on forgiving him or not I would suggest you to forgive him and give him a chance,it's not easy but with time it will show so it's your choice if you want to or not" I told him kissing his cheek softly.

"I love you princess,I'm gonna give him a chance but if he does anything stupid I'll kill him"

"Glad you chose the right"

....

So it's been 3 days and Zandy and Rick have been hanging out lately and their bond grew strong.

But I don't give a shit about that right now,I'm thinking about my BIRTHDAY that's in a weeekkkkkk!!!!

Guess who's excited???Im excitedd???Whos excited???Meeee

Ya I'll stop now,I think you guys are embarrassed for me right now.

Well yep it's almost my birthday guess who's turning 19?? Ya meeeeee,if I did not mention this before My Zandy is turning 20 like in 3 months.

Welp enough talking...

"YO BITCH WHERE YO UGLY ASS AT HOE???" I heard Madeline shout

This potatoe looking slut.

"IM IN HERE UGLY" I yell from my closet,hopefully she heard me because my closet is huge.

Her and Veronica came inside and groaned.

Da faaaaaaq?

"What?" I asked eyeing them weirdly

"Oh we missed you" they jumped on me and hugged me crushing my bones,I might have broke one if your wondering...

That's only if you were wondering!

"I missed my hoes too" I laughed and they glared

"Oh shut up"

"So where are the guys?" I asked I haven't seen Xander for like this whole morning until now,which is pretty weird considering the fact that he's always with me.

"O-oh um their in his office for the meetings place thing not his normal office ,he's sorting something out" Veronica said nervously and I eyed her suspiciously and Madeline nodded her head way too fast.

"I'm suspicious mhm,Can I go see him" I asked"No he does not want to be bothered"Maddie said "Too bad I'm going though" I said and ran to the direction of his meeting office

I opened the door as quickly as I can and ran inside but stopped when I saw more then 20 pairs of eyes staring at me.There were chefs,people who designed things and more people.?!

"Hehe...u-um hi" I waved nervously

Well isn't this awkward...

It sure is Ari it sure is...

"Princess what's wrong?" I snapped my head towards Xander."Oh you know haha,trying to look for you?" I said but it sounded abit more like a question

"Why were you looking for me?" "Well I didn't see you today so I just wanted to see you because I missed you and I wanted to see you again but...but I didn't know you were in a meeting so you know enough with me blabbering I'll just leave now" I said and right when I was gonna open the door to leave,I felt two hands grip my waist.

I turn around to Come faced to face to the one and only Xander.

"Nope your staying,did you have breakfast" I shook my head no because I was waiting for him to come.

"I was waiting for you Zandy"In the back I heard a series of 'aweeee' and then I blushed wrapping my hands around Zandy'

"Marthaaa" he called,Martha was one of the girls who helped around the pack.

"Yes Alpha?" She came in and asked"Please prepare two plates of breakfast for me and Ariel"

"Yes Alpha and future Luna" she then left

"Here come sit princess" he sat on the only chair left and placed me on his lap.

"Alpha do you want her to hear?" Someone asked

"Yes it doesn't matter but don't discuss the second subject" he said

" what's the subjuects?" I asked looking at Xander.

" the first one is the one where you become The Luna which is in 3 days and we just have a whole busy week,but I can't tell you one of the things,you'll figure that out soon though" Xander replied

"3 DAYSSS AND YOI TELL ME THIS NOW WHAT AM I GONNA WEAR,IM GONNA MEET SO MANY PEOPLE AND AND OMG WE HAVE TO DO SOMETHING" everyone in the room chuckled and Xander rolled his eyes.

"It's all taken care of Ariel stop being a drama queen" Parker said

He was here?oh ya and jay is here too mwhahaha,I'm random

"Oh hi Parker didn't see you there" I said smiling at him

"Wow,I feel the love" he muttered and I rolled my eyes.

"We already prepared the food and decoration we just need your dress Luna and Alphas suit" some guy around 25 said.

"Oh okay" I grinned "Princess everyone already know what their wearing,but were last because what we wear is most important,after that you'll be presented with a crown or a tiara I'll be needing a crown as well,we get it because we become like the power couple you know"he winked at the last part,while I giggled.

"When do we go shopping?"

"Today after we eat breakfast"

Right when he said that Martha Came in with our food.Lemme tell you I was drooling looking at what she brought.

I squealed and got up and jumped up and down skipping to Martha,everyone just stared.

"Thanks Martha!" I chirped and hugged the old lady what she's not actually that old she look like she's in her 30's good enough age for her.

"Y-your welcome Luna" she nodded and hugged me back and left the room.

"Lets eat!"i chirped but then remembered that everyone Here probably didn't eat.

"Wait..we can't eat they didn't eat" I said to Xander referring to everyone in the room

"Oh no Luna don't worry we all ate before we came you and Xander go and eat" The same 25 year old boy said.

Meh if they ate then okay.

Food here I come!!!

"Guys meetings over you may all leave now" Xander dismissed them and they all went out with a 'bye Alpha and Luna' they closed the door and left so it was only me and Zandy left.

"So shopping today" Xander said taking a bite out of his pancake while gulping down his cappuccino.

"Mhmm what about it" I said eating my waffle and helping my milk.

"Only me and you" he mumbled stuffing more food into his mouth.

"Yep,me and you and our bags that will soon join us" I replied

"Mhm now hurry and eat,shopping day today!" He said and drank more of his cappuccino.

....

Kay so that was the chapter for today I'll be updating double long chapters today because that's my apology for not updating in forever -coughs- a week

You saw that picture at the top? Yep that's supposed to be funny here's another one just to make ur day

Lots of love from Ya girl

Pinterest: ZBazziFollow me there

Chapter 16/Luna and birthday plans

Xander's p.o.v(you can love me later)

"Can't you hurry up???Im already done" I whine I swear girls take hours to get dressed she's been in her room for more then 30 minutes already and now she's telling me she's putting a bit of makeup on.

"Can't you shut up for once god damn ya ass need some patience" she called over the door from her room.I roll my eyes and sigh.

"Just hurry up"

"Boy!!your the one who told me we're going to buy me clothes and now your bothered wait till I'm done,I'm gonna hit you with my god damn lipstick liner" she yelled.

Oooh Spicy I likey

"I'm sorry princess,I'll be patient"Right when I said that she came out of her room looking stunning I told her to wear something comfortable,after shopping I'm taking her to get ice cream.

She has a good sense In fashion.

I was wearing ripped jeans and a white hoodie.

"I'm done are you happy?" She rolled her eyes while I glared,she looked at me and pouted.

"Don't roll your eyes at me"

"I can do what I want" she rolled her eyes again,I growled and she whimpered,I'm tryna show her who has power here.

"Ariel" I sighed and grabbed her arm embracing her and kissing her forehead.

"I'm Sowwy boo " she looked up at me and pouted.

I just want her so bad ugh!!

"It's okay sweetheart" I smiled and she blushed at the nickname I called her.

"Come on let's go" I said enterwining are fingers and taking her to the Ferrari.

We hoped in and I headed straight towards the biggest mall.

Ariel turned the radio on and Physco by post Malone started playing

"Hell yeah!!" I say and that my ladies and gentlemen is how me And my Princess started a musical.

We both started nodding are heads and started singing

"Damn, my AP goin' psycho, lil' mama bad like MichaelCan't really trust nobody with all this jewelry on youMy roof look like a no-show, got diamonds by the boatloadCome with the Tony Romo for clowns and all the bozos, My AP goin' psycho, lil' mama bad like MichaelCan't really trust nobody with all this jewelry on youMy roof look like a no-show, got diamonds by the boatloadDon't act like you my friend when I'm rollin' through my ends, though" we sang our hearts out and laughed.

"Okay this is my part shut up" she giggled and she started acting like she had a guitar.

"You stuck in the friend zone, I tell that four-five the fifth, ayHunnid bands inside my shorts, DeChino the shit, ayTry to stuff it all in, but it don't even fit, ayKnow that I been with the shits ever since a jit, ayI made my first million, I'm like, "Shit, this is it, " ay30 for a walkthrough, man, we had that bitch lit, ay" she sang then I joined when the song ended we laughed and arrived at the mall.

She was about to open the door when I growled and she looked at me and raised her hands in surrender,while I was walking to her side I was getting excited yet nervous thinking about the birthday plan I made with everyone that was in the meeting with me that day we were discussing that and the Luna ceremony.She does not know what's coming for her,I laughed at myself in my head while my wolf jack grinned and purred at the thought.

I opened her door and she got out and grinned.

"Shopping time!!!" She squealed and jumped up and down she grabbed my hand and dragged me inside.

"Okay first your dress and my tux" I dragged her into an expensive store that's filled with dresses and suits.

"Choose wich ever one catches your eye" I said and she chuckled.

We went around the store for five minutes when she ran towards the men section and pulled up a tux.

"Omg this would look great on you omg omg you have to try it on" she said and pulled me inside the changing room.

It fit perfectly and it honestly looked really hot on me,if I was a girl I would have added my dramatic hair flip but I'm not a girl so...*awkward silence*

I went out of the room and posed for her putting my hands in my pockets and I grinned.

"So?" I asked"It's perfect you look amazing,can we get you this one unless you don't like it" she said and smiled.

"Of course I want it,you chose it and I love anything you pick,my girl has a sense in fashion" I winked and she blushed

"I'm getting this one now come on we have to get you your dress,then crown and mine then our shoes" I said and went in the women's aisle.

We looked around when my eyes landed on the perfect dress.

An employee came and asked if we needed help."How may I help you Alpha?" She bowed her head down

"I want Ariel to try this on" I said pointing to the dress

"Yes one sec Alpha" she said and gave it to us and left.

Ariel grabbed it and looked at the tag

"3000$???" She gasped"no xander we can't take it it's too much"

"Nope,the price doesn't matter whatever looks nice and whatever you like or want we're getting anything you set your eyes on we're getting" I tell her and grabbed her hand.

"But-"

"No but or butts or boots okay?! We're getting it and that's final now how try it on" I said and pushed her inside the changing room.

5 minutes later she came out and my mouth fell open she looked absolutely stunning.

"You look gorgeous princess,we're definitely getting this" I said and she grinned and nodded while blushing and went back inside to change.

When she came out we grabbed the tux and dress and went and paid for them.

"Now it's shoes shopping,for the crowns I have an assistant who's gonna bring us the most expensive and luxurious ones now let's go get us some shoes" I exclaimed happily,I get so happy when I'm with her,shopping is the funnest with her because if she does not like something she starts saying how ugly it is and how it looks like it's from the 1970's but she only tells me that because she doesn't want people to hear her.

We went into the shoe shop and we found some nice shoes I got black ones that match my tux and she got beige heels

" that will be 1890$" the cashier said pushing her outfit down,while I rolled my eyes I looked at Ariel who was glaring at her and she had her middle finger out but was hiding it behind her back,I chuckled and payed.

We went out of the store when she started rambling.

"Did you not see that!!??She was eyeing you like she wants to eat you it was kinda scary! it's like she's actually put you on a plate,I swear if it weren't for my self respect I would have slapped that bitch a cross the face and put her in a freaking dungeon t-" She rambled it was cute but I had to stop her because we were at the shop for the personal made crowns so I kissed her and closed my eyes.

She kissed back and I pulled back when she pouted.

"No more for you princess we're here" I grinned and she shrugged

"Your loss" she replied and walked inside.

I just laughed and followed her

"Alpha Xander!!"Jarred called,he was the one who made the crowns

"Hi Jarred,the crowns are ready?" I asked and he nodded I grabbed Ariel's hand and she looked at everything with awe.

"So now what"she asked "He's gonna bring the crowns and then we're gonna look around the mall for fun" I said and she nodded her head and grinned.

"Here you go Alpha and Luna" he said Handing me two gold boxes one said Alpha the other said Luna.

I handed the one wich said Luna to My baby girl and I took the one that said Alpha obviously instead of one being called 'WORLD'S STRONGEST KILLER'

I opened the box and nodded my head in approval it was indeed really King like.I like it like that.

(Imagine it real like not plastic or some shit)

Ariel opened up hers and gasped"It's so prettyyyy,I love it" she said and giggle putting it on her head.

"How do I look" She was twirling around and winked

"You look stunning gem" I said "You and your nicknames" she mutters and I smirked

"Now lets go around the mall" I said grabbing her hand.

So we went into her favourite stores and she looked at a bunch of out-fits,why is she not getting anything?

"Why aren't you getting anything?" I frowned"I already used along of your money..and these are too expensive so it doesn't matter,let's just go back home"she said and tried getting out of the store.

Key word "she tried"

"No I already told you I'll buy you whatever you want I make a billion dollars everyday this is nothing compared to the amount of money I have"

A/N : I'm not even kidding imagine he gets a billion everyday I wish I was that rich da hell?Anyways back to the story sorry for interrupting your uh marvellous story

"A-are you sure?" She asked looking into my eyes

"Of course I'm sure here I'll even help you pick out outfits if you want"

"Okay!" She grinned,it gets me so happy seeing my mate this happy I'd do anything to keep that beautiful smile on her face and whoever makes her cry will suffer dearly her soul is made of pure and she's like a goddess.

We looked around all her favorite stores and we got a bunch of things she made me buy clothes and forced me to wear nice ones because apparently my clothes are always grey,white or black.

I got her everything she looked at.

Here are not even half the things we bought,I kind of told her if she doesn't buy anything I'll force her and give her The silent treatment oops.

Chapter 17/ Being Luna and surprises

A riel's p.o.v

Today is the day,I'm becoming Luna,hell yeah!

I woke up,pushed Xander off the bed ran to the washroom and then I did all of my business,the Ceremony was at 3 pm and Rn it was 11 pm so I had a couple of hours.

Xander came in the washroom,looking like a penguin because he's forcing himself to drag his feet,he sat on the toilet lid and groaned.

"I'm so freaking tired" he whined and rubbed his eyes.

"I wanna make face masks" I say giving him the 'you better do it with me ' look

"Let's do it my face gotta shine too" he replied making a girl voice.

He tried

I got my liquid mask cream and put it all over his face,he did the same with mine.

We looked like this:

We wait for 15 minutes until it's settled on our faces then I begin peeling mine off.

"Ow!How do you girls take this shit off?!! Ow! On my god what the f*ck???"

I looked at Him and just bursted our laughing.

"Here you go lemme help you" I say " what no your gonna freaking hurt my face" he said and turned his face around from me.

"No I'm not!!" I grabbed his face and ripped it off with force.

He screamed and glared at me.

I laugh and look at his faces shaped mask in my hands and show it to him.

"See it takes everything off" I said and threw it in the trash.

I wash my face and he washes his in the sink next to mine.

I go out go on my room,i take my pyjamas off and go in my closet.

I hear my door open and close,then Xander comes in.

"Princess where's my tux?" He asks,I'm still in my bra and underwear,he comes in and I squeal.

"It's on my couch go get it"

"Where are you?" He asks

"I'm in the closet but I'm only in my underwear and bra get out!!"

"Nope I can't miss out on a chance like this"

He comes in and walks inside to find me,I felt hands grab my waist and take me backwards.

"Gotcha" he whispered

I blushed and tried getting out of his grip.

"Xander I'm not wearing anything" I said

"Your beautiful" he murmured against my skin while caressing my back.

He nibbled on my ear and pressed light kisses all over my face.

"Go get dressed come on" I grin and drag him out of my closet and pass him his tux.

"Fine" he groaned and went out into his room.

I put the dress on with the help of Madeline and Veronica.

"Girl your becoming Luna" Veronica said adding sass to her voice on purpose.

"Right?!?" Madeline said and asked "Are you excited?"

"Hell yeah I am " I replied laughing.

"Ya we can tell,your the Mate of the strongest man out there and now everyone's at your feet"

" not because of that,it's just that I love being with him and I love him so makes everything better"

We kept chatting until they finished my hair and makeup.

We finished and we went downstairs,the ceremony was held in someplace close near.

I went downstairs and all eyes were on me. The eyes of my best friend and staff of course the Pack lived in the house in front,Xander said it would be better if only our group stayed here.

There's this one slut and her minions that try seducing my man to let them in and you know what happened after I saw that.

"Princess you look stunning"

"Awh boo and so do you" I laughed and kissed him,he wrapped his hands around my waist and I wrapped mine around his neck.

We pulled back for air and decided it was time to go.We all hoped into the limo and sat,laughed and talked until we arrived.

....

So it's my speech time and after that we're gonna be presented as Luna and Alpha,I mean he's already Alpha but you know I have to be presented as Luna so here I am talking to over then 7802 people.

"U-um hi" I wave,Xander standing beside me watching me with adoration.

"My name is Ariel McKnight and I'm Happy to be informed that I am Your L-Luna,I wanna make sure every one here is safe and happy,and not in danger and I'll be sure to be the best Luna in history" I say.

Everyone soon erupts in loud cheers and applauses,I see my parents there smiling and clapping.

'Good job honey' my mom mouths and winks with a thumbs up.

A guy comes forward with our crowns and puts them on our heads.

We heard a chorus of 'yasss'

Xander then looks at me,grabs my waist and slams his lips onto mine,we move them in sync moving them not caring if people are staring.

Who cares,they have a free reality show.

We pull back and look to see everyone grinning,some girls with looks of jealousy.

Sike bitches he's mine so too bad*adds dramatic hair flip*

....

Xander's p.o.v

I watch as people greet Ariel and she gives them a big smile shaking their hands

Soon the ceremony was over and everyone went back home,when we arrived I tell Ariel I'll be in my office,and head there.

I sat down in my desk,it was 7 pm right now and I was writing my ideas and plans for her birthday in a journal,that journal is literally about her only,what I wanna do for her,get her,her favourite things and everything.

I write down what I'm doing,I'm gonna be putting random gifts I get for her everyday until her birthday,that's in a week,on the actual day I'm making her a huge ass bomb birthday party I heard that she's never had a really party because no one liked her everyone though she was 'sassy'.

Starting from tomorrow I'm starting my plan I'm gonna head to the mall first thing when I wake up and then I'll proceed with the plan for the past week,this week is gonna be her best week.

I close the journal and place it in my drawer,I check my phone and look At my notes I have all her food orders from like Starbucks,McDon-

alds,Wendy's,Subway,Tim Horton's,In and Out etc...I'm boyfriend material.

"No your not" jack my wolf said.

I rolled my eyes and went downstairs to grab nachos and water,I'm guessing
Ariel would be watching Netflix in her room,I went inside and to my guess
I was right.

"Awhhh my baby come here" she said,I went to her and she looked at me
weirdly and took the nachos.

"What about me?"i pouted

"You can massage my back" she replied shrugging "no I'm kidding sit,eat
and watch" she said

"Okay but do you still want the massage?" I asked

"I mean if you want"

I'm taking that as a yea

She was sleeping on her stomach and watching the tv while eating nachos.

I start massaging her back for like 10 minutes then I hear light snores.

Wtf she's already asleep?

Awhhh ma baby.

I take her bridal style,put her under her bed covers and I take off my
shirt,leaving me in my shorts and then I go under the covers and fall into
sleep.

I love this girl so much.

Chapter 18/A day before the Birthday

IMPORTANT NOTE There might be a lot of pictures representing how things look so please don't comment on how there's too much pics in this chapter I already know but that's how i do it sometimes in my book but if you don't like pics then wait for the next chapter which is tomorrow ,thanks lots of love)THERES STILL A STORY SO READ IF YOU DONT WANT TO WAIT FOR THE NEXT CHAPTER(MORE THEN 10 pics I REPEAT MORE THEN 10 PICS)

....

Xander's p.o.v

I wake up and turn around to find Ariel sleeping peacefully,I sigh how did I get this lucky?

I look at her soft features and grin,she's beautiful no one can compare to her.

I kiss her forehead and get out of bed slowly so I won't wake her up and head to the washroom.I do my business and wash my hands then brush my teeth and get out.

I went inside my closet and picked out a casual outfit.Which considered ripped black jeans a army green shirt and black vans.I went downstairs and told one of the maids to prepare breakfast for Ariel when she wakes up.

I went into my Lamborghini,then drove off to the flower shop,I went in and I customized the perfect ones and put it in a a silver diamond box.

I went to the mall which was pretty close to the bouquet of flowers shop,I went inside and got so much things,I had 3 of my butlers come with me so they can put everything in the limo ,the stuff took a lot of space litterly the whole limo.

I went back home with the limo following and made sure everything was good.I put everything in a huge room no one goes inside it.

I go back upstairs with a 3 presents to give to Ariel for today but tomorrow will be the big day.Shes turning 19 it's a big deal if you ask me.For her birthday tomorrow I have the perfect plan,I invited her family and mine.Theres more people coming.Ive been giving her so much gifts this past week,I gave her jewelry,shoes,clothes,makeup,stuffed animals and even food.

She always said thanks.

So I open the door to her room because she must be in there,it's been 4 hours since I left and I'm pretty sure she wouldn't be sleeping in my room that long.

I go in and find her colouring in the colouring book I gave her with the bunch of crayons and markers I got her.

I got her those with the outfits and shit but here are some other things I got her.

- -

I chuckled at her position she's on the floor and when she hears me,she looks up and smiles.

"Hey" she says and closes the marker."Hi princess" I reply and walk towards her,she gets up and jumps on me before she jumps I put the small little gifts next to the door.

She jumps on me and I catch her.

"I missed you so so so much" she said and she nuzzled her head in the crook of my neck and inhaled my scent.

"I missed you too babe" I said kissed her cheeks.

"Lets colour" she grinned,looking into my eyes.

"Nope first I have your last presents for the week,I mean before your actual birthday" I said and put her down so I can grab her gifts.

"Hey" she pouted"you already got me enough I would have been alright with just like a perfume." She said and I rolled my eyes.

"No,no and no,your gonna have to get used to it cause it's gonna be happening a lot whether you like it or not,and anyways you get me things too like you buy clothes and shoes so that's fair." I say and she puts a strand of her hair behind her ear.

"I love you" she says

"And I love you more" I smile.

Ariel's p.o.v

I look at my amazing mate and smile hard.He's so cute anyone would be lucky to have him.

He goes next to the door and pulls a couple things up.

"Okay sit on the bed and close your eyes" he said and dragged me to the bed.

I close my eyes and hear ruffling,then I hear him say 'here we go'

I felt the bed moving,then he told me to open my eyes.

"Okay open your eyes" he said,I opened them and he pointed to my side and I gasped at what I saw.

And another one like that but with different and more makeup and small perfumes.

I look to my side to find the two bags I wanted the most,I told him that I liked it so much,I didn't buy it because I didn't have time.

And last but not least there was a candy LOOKING FUDGING CAKE.

"Is this my birthday cake?" I asked with a smile looking at it.

"Oh no of course not my lady" he replied with a British accent.I don't know why he hides it like his dad is half British so he speaks in that kind of accent but his mom is American.

His voice is so hot when he talks with his accent.

"Awhhh thank you" I cried,yes actually cried because if someone was buying presents this whole week and still said they bring you presents on your
birthday I'd guarantee you you'd be happy.

Unless your some gold digger that appreciates nothing but shit then ya.

"Awhh why are you crying,don't cry" he said and hugged me.

I squeezed him so hard I thought I killed him for a second.

I put everything at the side where the other gifts are,I decided it would be
nice if I put every gift I got to the side and then looked at them on my
birthday,well except for the markers that is.

"Wanna go out for dinner?" Zandy asked,and I nodded.

....

Xander left 30 minutes ago so I can get dressed,Madeline is with me but
not Veronica because she's out with lover boy.

Maddie was doing my hair and makeup and when she finished I was
impressed.

"Zaymmmm girl if I were a boy I'd tap that" she playfully winked.

I walked to my long mirror and check the whole outfit with the makeup.

"Damn I look hot" I laughed

"Ya he better think so too" She replied,laughing.

"Thanks boo" i kissed her cheek and she winked."I'm all about that fashion"
she said doing a hair flip.

I laugh and go in my closet to grab my heels,I go back out and hold them,I head downstairs to find Nutella on a toast,I mean it's 7 pm who's gonna eat it at that time?

Ha me?!

I go towards it and watch around to see if someone's there's I quickly shove it in my mouth and go towards the sink to wash around my mouth.

I get out of the kitchen and sit down in the living room ,scrolling through my phone,I hear the door open and I look up to see Xander.

"Come on princess" he says and grabs my hand and escorts me outside.

We go inside a limo and I sit down next to Xander.

"Tomorrow's your birthday" he sang

"Yes it's my birthday" I said laughing,he enterwined our fingers and kissed me with all his mighty and I kissed back with the same passion.

Soon after we arrived,he opened the door to the fast food restaurant and we entered,we took our seats and chatted until the waiter or waitress came.

"Hello what can I get you?"a waiter that looked to be in his 30s asked.

"Can I get chicken breasts,chicken wings and just chicken about 20 piece in total,a extra large fries,2 lemonades,And cheese sticks 20 pieces" Xander said.

"Um can you please add some ketchup,mayo and chipoli sauce" I asked

"Yes of course,your order will be given to you in 5 to 10 minutes" he said and left.

You might ask who eats that much?

The answer is me and Xander,it's what food lovers do you know,its a thing.I think...meh anyways.

Xander made a lot of jokes while we were waiting for the food,that's how I almost died because of me laughing.

The waiter came with our food and then we started eating.

I only 5 cheese sticks..OH WHO AM I KIDDING I ATE THEM ALL BECAUSE THEY TASTE GOOD!

We get up paying the whole bill,then getting upTo leave.We arrive home and I head up inside my room to sleep.Xander is gonna be up a little late so he told me not to wait.I gave him a hug and a peck.I went upstairs and entered my room,I changed my clothes and fell asleep.

....

Xander's p.o.v

So the guys and girls are helping me set up the house for when she wakes up now there's pink,silver,blue and gold balloons all over the ceiling,the maids are doing the dining room and the food,I then sneak In Ariel's room,I bring everything I bought I put some in front of her bed,then the two sides of her bed and I put a bunch of balloons on the top and some roses next to her.

I finish up and sneak back out,I go downstairs and find Maddie and Veronica preparing the gifts table and I look to see jay and Parker preparing where the food will be only 100 people will be there.

When we finish up outside too it's already 1 am so we all head to sleep.

....

Ariel's p.o.v

I roll to my side and groan,the light hitting my eyes I get up and gasp at the sight,I hear a chuckle next to me and find Xander sitting beside my bed grinning.

"Surprise?" He said

"Oh my god" I say

There was everything sitting there,I'm in shock right now,this is birthday goals.

That's how in my room on my bed,in the house,ya I'll stop now.

That's how the things on my bed were placed and I'm wondering how I didn't kick them off,and there was balloons.Then the side of my beds and in front if it.

Left side^

Right side ^

In front^ then I got next to the door where there's a table with a bunch of Victoria secret and pink bags with a heart box and roses inside and to the side some Nutella and kinder eggs.

And next to it there was balloons with I love you and happy birthday.

I launched at him and engulfed him in a hug

"Oh my lorrdddd thank youuu!" I say ha most likely shouted.

"Anything for this queen" he said pointing at me,he kissed my lips in a sweet tender way,soon pulled back.

"There's still more to the surprise,go get dressed" he said

I ran to my closet and picked out my birthday outfit.

It was a nice light pink short dress,I curled my hair and put it down and I did light makeup.

Xander was next to me,he grabbed my hand and led me out of my room there was confetti all over the floor and there were banners and pictures of me.

Damnnn,no comment it's too good to be true.

I look around when I'm downstairs and there's people sitting on the couches everywhere and there's little kids talking,I look at the table and find a bunch of gifts sprawled everywhere,more like 100 or so gifts.

"Hello everyone we're here for my princess is birthday and she's your Luna Ariel McKnight!Were gonna cut the cake,open presents then go outside and have fun" Xander announces catching everyone's attention.

Everyone nodded and clapped,we all sat in the dinning room ready to cut my cake,I looked over and saw a beautiful cake.

I lick my lips looking at the cake.

"Happy birthday To you,happy birthday to you" everyone started singing,when everyone stopped singing I blew the candles.

We all sat down and started eating a slice and eating food.

"So you like the party?" Xander asked

"Like it? I freaking love it!" I said and laughed.

He laughed too and wrapped his arm around my shoulders.

"Okay time to open presents!!" Veronica shouted,oh ya Veronica's here.

Everyone's heads to the living room and takes a seat,I sit next to the table of presents.

"Mine is last!"Maddie shouted

"Mine is with Maddie " Veronica shouted as well.

I opened all the presents except jays and Parker's,Maddie and Veronica,my parents,Xander's parents and Xander's,ya apparently he has one more small presents like who can afford all this.

Him he's a billionaire.

I start by opening jays and Parker's,jay got me a teddy bear with chocolates and a whole kit of nail polish Parker got me earrings and chokers,pyjamas .Xanders parents gave me makeup,and 2 art kits.My parents got me things from pink and Victoria secret.

Then I open Maddie and Veronica's,they got me things from lush and some perfumes from pink.

"Awhhhh thanks all of you" I saw and hug all of them.

They hug back and kiss my cheek.

"It's Xander's last present now out of all 17833 he got you,he's still got more" my mom said over reacting on the number,Xander just laughed.

I open the box he put his present in and open it up while everyone is watching,I open it up and smile,it's a diamond like box and roses with a necklace in the middle.

The necklace had a heart with the first letters of our names.I hugged him and kissed him,I heard laughs and ooohs.

"Okay kids not PDA" Madeline said

We all laugh then we head outside,2 hours later the party ends and maids begin to clean.

I go up to my mom and hug her.

"We should have a girls day mom,I miss you" I said and hugged her tight.

"Ya we should" she said and winked.

"I'll text you when" she added I nodded and she left with Xander's parents and my dad.

I go to the dining room and take everything up to my room with the help of 2 maids and 2 butlers of course,I place everything where I want it to be.Xander made my room way bigger because he though the other was too small for my things and me to be in there,so he added a pretty rose gold and silver bed with a bunch of cute pillows and a bunch of more classy room stuff.

I finish up placing every single thing in my room and change my pyjamas,I brush my teeth and brush my hair.

I get out of my room and go into Xander's to find him already under the covers scrolling through his phone,I jump on him and roll to the side,then I go under the blankets,I grab my phone and scroll to it to.

"Hey Zandy?" I called,looking at Xander,he looked at me and smiled.He put our phones on his nightstand.

"Yes Ari?" He asked

"I love you" I said and hug his torso laying my head on his chest.

"And I love you more" he grinned and kissed the crown of my head "I can't get used to you saying that because I want you to tell me every single day" he smiled and kissed my lips.

I giggle and close my eyes.

"Go to sleep flower" he whispered and kissed my cheek,he put his head On the pillow and we both fell into darkness.

....

2662 words??? Zaymmmmm Daniel.That's a first.

Vote,comment and DONT BE A SILENT READER, COMMENT AND ILL GIVE YOU FOOD YES CALL ME DESPERATE.

Shut up and don't complain that I was long on updating okay?? I GAVE U A LONG CHAPTER!!!

Now if you'll excuse me I have another story's chapter to write pceeee- SUMMER BREAK IS IN A WEEK SO ILL ACTUALLY BE UPDATING YAAAY

Chapter 19/ Salons ,Arcades and being a good boyfriend

Ariel's p.o.v

I wake up next to Xander,cuddled up next to me,I stare at his face in awe and suddenly his eyes shot open.

"Hey" he murmurs smiling at me,our faces were close and our noses were almost touching.

"Hi" I whisper,and smile back.

This would be freaking couple goals,not even kidding.thats probably how me and buddy boy here would look like.

I kiss his cheek then move to his lips,I kiss them then try to get up.

Ya keyword try because I didn't move a centimetre.

"Xander come on I need to go get dressed"

"Nooo" he whined

"Come on" I said pulling myself up,he groaned and got up.

"Hey why are you getting dressed anyways?" He asked wearing his slippers following me to the washroom.

"Um did you forget?You told me we're going to the arcade with Maddie,Veronica and the guys" I replied and started to brush my teeth.

"Oh ya and I told you I'm taking you to the nail salon,I saw how you always looked at your nails" he said,damn he notices every movement I do,that's kind creepy though if you think about it.

"Yay!Okay lets go then" I get out of the washroom with him trailing behind me like a lost puppy.

I go in his closet and pick an outfit.Yes I keep a outfit in there in case I'm too lazy to go to my room which is in front of his room.I Wear a casual outfit.

I go sit on the chair in front of his vanity I put some makeup in one his drawers because I sleep in his room at times.

"Don't wear makeup" Xander tells me and looks at me.

"Why"

"Because you don't freaking need it,your face is beautiful the way it is,please other bimbos need it but not you because your stunning"he said looking at me with love.I awed at him.

"Awh thanks boo,but I just do it because I enjoy it" I said "but if you don't want me to add right now I won't " I continued and just applied lip gloss.

We finish and head downstairs,all I'm thinking about is Christmas it's soon and I'm excited.Its like in a week.Me and the girls are going Christmas shopping tomorrow and I'll ask Xander later if I can buy decorations for my room,his and the mansion.

Oh shit I forgot my purse,I run upstairs to my room,oh ya you know how I said Xander renovated my room because apparently too small when it was bigger then my own house?Ya it actually looked nice and I loved it.

That's only the bed fam not even the whole room,he got me pillows that represented my style,no I'm not picky it's just what I prefer because I have a life and actual likings to things.

A girl gotta love her mans for buying her pillows am I right? No I'm the only one?Ya imma stop because y'all don't seem interested we'll do you want a tour around my room,is this what people want?

I only know YouTubers do this kinda tour things,I'll do it too.

Lemme start off by my vanity's,my amazing good looking vanity's.He had placed a lot of vanity's in my room and expanded because the things I got can't all fit in the "small" room I used to have.So I legit had 5 huge cubicals and one huge vanity.

The cubicals for my things.

He put me that one because I'm that crafty extra girl.

Well ya then last but not least my normal vanity with all my makeup on it.

I had a huge walk in closet and a huge washroom too,I go in my closet and grab a bag instead of a purse because we're going to an arcade for God's sake.And to A salon!

I go downstairs and find everyone ready next to the door.

"Oh finally,I swear I could walk to new York and back and still you'd be up in your room trying to find a bag" Parker said making me roll my eyes.

"Stop over reacting hoe" I reply and everyone laughs.

We all head out but go in different cars.Well meet up there but Xander told them we're going to the salon.

I'm with Xander jamming to only you by little mix and cheap codes.

I freaking love it.

Just like I love food,and Xander and Nutella and makeup and ya..sorry

We arrive and get out.

I go in and enter,a lady comes up with her shirt half way down her boobs,dressed in a small skirt and small shirt.

I roll my eyes and do something crazy or weird only I would o I pull her shirt up so it's covering the exposed parts of her breast,she looks at me shocked and I give a fake smile.

"Your very welcome"

She looked so embarrassed.Xander laughed so hard he was crouching and holding his stomach.

"S-sorry,I'll be right with you,f-follow me" She stuttered.

That's what I freaking thought hoe!

I sit down in the nice pretty salon.

I sit down and she passes me an acrylic nail book.

"Would you like any of these?" She asked with a smile.

"Id like to tell you what I want please,none of these come to my liking." I said and she nodded,I tell her how I want my nails.While she's doing that

Xander is there doing faces at me,faces sticking his tongue out I found that cute,am I the only one?

She finished and I looked at them,oooh la la,me like,I laugh in my head because of me being stupid.

Xander came next to me,and I showed him them posing and winking.

We both laughed,then the nail worker talked.

Thanks mate.

"We have a bunch of fake acrylic nail kits each for 16$ we have a whole pack of em for 78$,would you like to buy one kit or the pack?" I was about to say no when Xander cut me off.

Rude much.

"Sure we'll take it" he replied taking out cash out of his wallet,he took out a 100$ bill and gave it to her.

"Okay I'll be right back" she wandered off.

"Why would you say yes?"

"First,it's a good deal,second your gonna have to be used to this already I'll be doing it legit almost everyday,third because your a princess,my princess and I love you"

Wtf I'm a queen,I'm kidding don't eat me.

I didn't protest because there's no use,he'll be doing it often he won't listen if I tell him not to give me anything,it's like a Hobby to him.

"I love you too" I mumbled,blushing and looking away from him.

He chuckled and grabbed my chin and smashed his lips to mine,we moved them in sync when we hear heels clicking towards us,we pull a part and see the girl with the fake acrylics.

She hands them to Xander and he passes them to me I hold them and look at them ,their all my style.

We head out and I jump on his back and he almost trips that's the funny part.

Ha.ha I'm so funny.

We arrive and find the squad we go and find them.

"Finally!!" Jay said and came up to us with everyone else trailing behind.

We all head in the arcade and I wanted to play laser tag,I was about to ask when Parker beat me to it.

"Yo lets go laser tagging first"

"Ya" everyone agrees we all head to the entrance and everyone entered.

"Okay boys be girls" Madeline said

"Ya lets go" I say we pick the colour red and the boys green.

We enter the stadium and run off,I hide in a corner when I see a green light in the ceiling,that's to take away all the points from the green team and puts all the points to me,so I just sat in the corner shooting it and earning all the points.

Then suddenly a shadow appeared,I look to find Xander there,he's about to shoot me when I do 5 ninja rolls in a row.

"I don't think so buddy boy" I say and run I start shooting parker and jay,they were shooting Veronica and Madeline.

Mwahhhahah I'm so freaking evil,well I don't think saving my team is evil but shooting two people at a time and making them run for their lives is.

I laugh and I heard a beep coming from me,someone shot me,I turn around and see Xander holding the same smirk.

I aim at him and shoot 2748392 times in a row.

I go and run back to where the green light is and shoot it multiple times.

My suit soon turns off meaning the game ended,we head out to see who won first place,we go and guess who it is?!!

Yes meeee.

No I wish,it's Xander my dreams have all just fell.

I was second,jay was third the others came after.

"Ha see who won" Xander bragged,i stuck my middle finger at him and he laughed.

"Awh is my baby mad at me for winning" he said and pinched my cheeks.

"Nope" I said and licked his hand,serves him right.

We all started playing arcade games and I look at Xander and he had a whole bag of tickets and the bag is huge I'm telling you.

"What the hell?!!" I yelled

"What?"

"How did you get all that"

"I won them,but some other girls came up to me and gave me them for no reason,I mean they were flirting but I told them your my mate and I kinda punched one for not understanding and touching me" he shrugged.

I laughed and hugged him

"I love you" I tell him

"And I love you,how many tickets do you have?"he asked

"26" I murmured.

And that's when it happen he fell on the floor laughing.

I glare at him and he stands up and wipes his tears.

I roll my eyes and he hugs me.

"Don't worry I'll share" he grinned

"Hmmm"

.........................I'm outside with the girls sitting down,because we have are tickets to the guys because we legit had nothing.

Right now their getting their prizes.

"Ya so we going shopping for a bunch of Christmas shit tomorrow?" Maddie asked,eating iced slush we got all three of us.

We got some for the boys because we're not heartless.

"Ya,I'm gonna tell Xander" I tell her taking a scoop of the slush.

"I already told Parker he said yes" Veronica said.

"Same for jay" Madeline said.

We continued talking and eating until the boys came.

All their hands behind their backs.

" I got you something" Xander said and took out two stuffed toys.

I look at them in awe,it's a Mickey Mouse and Minnie Mouse.

I started giggling,he actually wasted his tickets on getting this for me.

"Do you like them?"

"I love them" I said and kissed him.

The other boys got small teddy bears for their girls,it's actually cute when you think about it.

We sit down and all eat our slush our yummy slush.

Our blue ocean like slush.

I'm weird like that.

"Hey Zandy?"

"Ya princess?" He says and shoves slush in his mouth looking at me.

"the girls are going Christmas shopping tomorrow,can I go with them?" I ask

"Ya of course,but be careful okay?"

"Ya,thank you" I say and side hug him

"No problem,thinking about it me and the guys might go too but different places and not where your going" he said

"That's fine with me" I grin

Xander's p.o.v

Thinking about Christmas,the boys and I have to go too,we have to get the girls presents and I have to buy things and wrap em up.

By now you should now how extra I go when stuff like these come up.

I go wayyy extra.

This year is gonna be fun all because of my princess.

....

Hey again,well seems like this guy likes to spoil his girl too.

Did you like this chapter??

I loved it

I'll be updating twice today just to make you guys adore me

-flips hair-

Byeee for noww

Chapter 20/ Christmas shopping and Chritmas balls.

A riel's p.o.v

I'm up and awake!

I'm going into Xander's room,I made breakfast and I wanna eat so I'm waking him up.

I go in and don't find him there,his bed is neat,so I go look in his office and there he is sitting down gulping his coffee going through his computer,he doesn't notice me.

I'm gonna cry now.

No I'm not.

"Xander"

"Princess!!I missed you!" He ran towards me and threw me in the air.

I believe I can fly!!

I giggle and he puts me down

"You saw me this morning" I say and he smiles.

"Ya but still" he winkes,I laugh and I grab his face.

"I made breakfast" I say tracing his perfect jawline.

"Let's go eat then,oh ya and I almost forgot there's a Christmas ball being held your coming with me" he says.

"You didn't even ask" I roll my eyes playfully,he shrugged and held my waist.

"I don't need to ask because you'll say yes anyways" he said.

"True,true" I nodded agreeing with him.

I drag him downstairs and into the kitchen,we sit down a began eating the breakfast I made.

Today I'm going Christmas shopping with the girls.

I finished my plate and took Xander's too when he finished,he hugged me and kissed my bye and told me to be careful,I was already dressed.

Me and the girls head out and I take Xander's car.

....

Me and the girls are at the mall,we enter Armani.

I look around and a watch catches my eye.

"Hey would you like the watch?" A guy behind the counter of glass said.

"Ya,and can I have the one next to it" I said politely,he nodded and took them out.The one next to it was nice too. It was navy.

I got him black Ana navy because he always wears those kind of coloured suits.

I buy the watches,the total was 680$ were 340$ each.

I buy him clothes and shoes.

I wanted to get him something that he would adore.

Me and the girls head out chatting and enter the customization bracelets shop.

I get a bracelet or him with my name on it.

You know so if a hoe comes up to him and sees that she'll be like.

Oooh bye.

But I guarantee they would care less.

Anyways we buy everything and head back.

....

Xander's p.o.v

I'm in my office on my computer dealing with pack business.

I decide to go let my wolf out because I haven't done that for a while.

I go outside and let jack take over.

....

I finish running after an hour and head back to my office.I go in google and search up...

What nice gifts to get your girlfriend.

Cute things girls like.

Tumblr girl gifts.

Yes I know what tumblr is,and I even know what Pinterest is,Ariel is always on them on her phone.

I find a bunch of things and note them down in my notebook that I have for her.

I can't wait to marry this girl,have kids,spoil each one of them and my amazing wife.

I want 4 kids to say the least.

2 boys,2 girls.

I want the girls to be twins that would be adorable and the boys I don't care what I just hope they will be healthy.

Why am I saying this she's not even pregnant.

'She will be in a month' jack said

'What do you mean?' I reply

'You clueless idiot,we'll have to mate eventually,she'll get heat and when will you mark her?I want her to be immortal like us!when you mark her she will be immortal! We're half vampire anyways' he says and I'm shocked to say the least,my mom and dad are both mates but the moon goddess chose a vampire to be mates to my dad.

I love my parents.

So now as you can tell I'm half and half,I'll tell Ariel soon.

'Ya she'll go through heat..and we have to mate unless she'll be in a lot of pain' I reply thinking about it. After that she'll become pregnant.

I sigh and lean back further into my chair,I still need a girls advice on what to get more things for Ariel.

I mind link Parker and jay and tell them I need to talk to their girls.

They reply with an ok and then Madeline and Veronica come in.

Madeline plops down on the leather seat in front of my desk.

"What's up fam?" She asks and puts her legs on my desk,I glare at her and push her legs off,Madeline laughs and sits next to her.

"I need help buying and finding more gifts for Ariel" I say and they both look at each other smirking.

Me and the guys already went to the mall,we bought a bunch of things and I ordered things from online but I want a gift that will also make her fill up with joy.

"Well,puppy"

I stare at the both of them confused.

"Say what now?" I said

"Buy her a puppy,she loves them and always wanted one" Madeline said and I nodded.

"Ya you can also buy her cute things from her favourite places,she'll love anything you eat her she loves you" Veronica continued,I took notes of everything and I nodded.

"Thanks you can leave"I said and they both saluted me like little girls and left.........I head in my car and go to the vet shop.

I look around and go to where the dogs are and find the perfect one!

I buy it and leave with it.

I put it outside in the backyard and place it in a dog house with food and water.

I go inside and go upstairs inside my room to find Ariel in my closet taking......

My hoodies,she took like 5 of them and turned around,she screamed when she saw me standing there watching her in amusement.

So f*cking cute.

"What are you doing?" I ask

"Umm...taking your hoodies?"

"Why?"

"Okay because they smell like you!There big and comfortable and I love them!" She says and I smirk.

I go towards her and grab her,putting my hands under her armpits,lifting her off the ground,she shrieked and clunged herself to me.

"I give you the right to take them" I kiss her and she kissed back with love and lust.She wraps her legs around my waist and puts her hand in my hair tugging it making me groan.

We go and lay on my bed cuddled up and she plays a movie.

I'm thinking about all the things I do for her yet nothing is enough.

I will buy her and do whatever she wants me to do. Or get.

I rest my head on her chest and she plays with my hair.

Soon we both drift into amazing sleep.

....

Yes I updated!!! Be happy and give me food!!

Anyways yes SUMMER BREAK IS HERE HOESSS AND I GET TO UPDATE NOT ONCE BUT TWICE??!!

YOU KNOW WHY!? BECAUSE IM FLIPPING AWESOME.

-claps- thank you thank you.

See ya tomorrow!!

Pce!

Chapter 21/ Dancing and Chritmas preperations

A riel's p.o.v

Right now,I'm sitting on my bed drawing a picture of me and Xander,I'm doing it so I can wrap it up as well and give it to him.

I colour it with the markers Xander got me for my birthday.

I finish it up and smile at it. I did pretty good.

This masterpiece!

I grab a small box and place it in it and then I wrap it in gold wrapping paper.

I put it with the 39 other gifts I got him,well now it's 40.

I get out of my room and go inside Xander's office.

He has his headphones in and he's listening to Wait by maroon 5.

How do I know??

Because it's blasting and you can hear all the way from South Korea. And I love that song so it's all good you know what I mean?

I mean I love South Korea and all those Kpop bands like BTS,JYJ,Exo,Bigbang,Kard and got7 etc...

I go around his table and sit on his lap.

He looks at me and smiles,I take his earphones out of his phone and he groans.

"Hey" he whined,I smirk and connect it to the speaker he has.

"Can I see your phone for a second" I say and he nods handing me it"sure".

I grab it and replay the song wait and blast the music,I grab him,and drag him to the middle of his big office there's a lot of space and so I try to twirl him around.

Soon the door opens and Parker,Jay , Veronica and Madeline walk in dancing.

"I'm joining the fun!"jay yells because of the loud music and started dancing with the others.

"This is so fun" Veronica yells and twirls around,Parker smirks at her and grabs her hand twirling her even more.

Madeline and Jay are Dancing together and me and Xander well he's twirling me around and we're all singing to the song.

"Oh, let me apologizeI'll make up, make up, make up, make up for all those timesYour love, I don't wanna loseI'm beggin', beggin', beginn', beggin', I'm begging youWait, can you turn around, can you turn around?Just wait, can we work this out, can we work this out?Just wait, can you come here please? 'Cause I want to be with you" we all sing and laugh.

After we played a bunch of other songs we all fall to the floor panting and laughing at Jay who looks like a worm on the floor.

We get up and go downstairs sitting on the couches.

"Are we going anywhere after Christmas Day?" Madeline asked looking at Xander because we always need his permission,well not me because I'm Luna.

No I'm kidding I have to ask or else I'll end up being glared at and yelled at by Xander.

Trust me it happened once and I started balling my eyes out and he apologized right when I started crying that time I stuck the middle finger at him for being a jerk.

Ya,but me and him have arguments some times but if we do,we can't go to sleep without solving it legit,he hates arguing with me the most because he hates seeing me sad.

"Ya were going on a cruise only us six" Xander replied drinking a coffee.

"Ya,we planned that it will go from La to this one clear beach and it's like bora bora but not bora bora,you know?" Parker said and we nod our heads.

Then Madeline shoots up from her seat and we all stare at her.

"Da Frik?" I say and look at her.

"WE'RE GOING ON A CRUISE!!!" She squeals and jumps back on the couch.

"Hell ya we are!" Veronica yells and I grin and clap my hands.

....

Me and the girls are up in Veronica's room right now.

"So what you guys wanna do?" I ask

"I know,you know how we're mated to the guys and everything?!" Veronica says excited grinning like a child.

"Ya?" Me and Madeline reply.

"We can make lists of dates and things to do with them,like fun things " she grins and I think about it.

"Your right,that would be nice" I say and Madeline nods.

Veronica gets lined papers and pencils and we start writing.

Soon after I had a couple lists,I finsh.

We all finished.

"Look what I wrote" I said showing them one of mine.

"Oooh look at mine" Veronica squeals and shows us hers.

....

Since Christmas is in two days I wanna decorate with Xander we already decorated the house but I wanted to add a Christmas tree in my room with decor.

"XANDER!!" I shout out,looking for him.

"Yes!!Im in your room!" He says and I run to my room and talking about Christmas trees there's one right there.

There's a big box next to him as well.

"What's all this?" I say closing my room door and walking towards him.

"I'm putting up a tree for you what else?" He says raising his eyebrow smirking at me.

Facepalm.

"Can I help?!" I chirp and he smiles " of course princess,it's your room" he said and I nodded sitting on the floor next to him he already added some deco to the tree.

While I add the decorations on the tree,he puts up my lights.

I look to the other side of my room which is like 7 meters away.

Yes my room is that big.

And see another tree.

I just saw that.

"Why is there another tree in my room?" I ask looking at Xander who looks down at me from the small later he has.

"Oh because there won't be a lot of space if I put you one tree" he said

"Ya but we're already also using the tree downstairs" I say

"Ya but don't argue,you need 3 trees and I don't care" he said and glared.

"Xander"I said I wanted to bake cookies with him, and I hate when he glares at me,it makes me so mad and makes me feel like I'm the one with no say in this part.

"Ariel I said don't argue,I love doing these kind of things for you!" He yelled

"I-I'm not arguing why do you have to be so mean sometimes,I was just gonna ask you something" I yelled,walking out of the room,into the wash-room outside.

Am I being dramatic?

Yes I just wanna see what he'll do if I ever get this mad at him,hehe i know I'm evil.

"Ariel,I'm sorry please get out your right I blamed you for no reason I don't want you to be mad at me before Christmas"

Awee my heart.

I unlock the door and look at him and grin.

"You we're acting weren't you?" He said eyeing me suspiciously.

I nodded and ran but before I move he catches me and takes me to the room.

I'm back to decorations,and he's helping me.

....

"Xander! That's not how!" I scold Xander.

We're making cookies but Xander doesn't know how to add icing.

"Well then please teach me,I'm trying to do my own design here" he says and adds way too much icing.

"Xander!!"

"Fine Fine"

I show him how and explain how he needs to do them.

Soon we both finish up a bunch of cookies.

"Do you see this masterpiece?!" Xander exclaims,taking a picture of it and posting it on insta and snap.

"I sure do,something made by MY hands" I say and smirk looking at him and his hung opened mouth.

"Your just jealous I do shit better then you" he said smirking back.

"Whatever helps your ego" I reply and he glared playfully.

....

I go in my room because it's 10 pm and wear my comfy winter pyjamas.

I tie my hair in a ponytail and go inside Xander's room with my phone and a bag of sour patch.

He's in his closet looking for a pyjama.

He grabs a black t-shirt and black and red pyjamas.

He takes his shirt off and I look at his 8 pack and v line oof. Just oof.

He puts his t-shirt on and I head out and flop on his bed waiting for him under his covers.

He comes in the room and smirks.

"Why hello" he says and goes under his covers pulling me between his legs.

He grabs the tv remote and turns the big platform tv and he grabs his controller for his ps4 or Xbox 1 I don't know he has like 4 of those.

He turns it on and plays Fortnite.

All these god damn boys be playing this,and even girls.

A/N(one of those girls being me -cough -cough)

His arms are wrapped around me while holding his controller and I just sit and watch him eating the sour patch gummies and stuffing some in my mouth and his mouth.

I finsh the bag and try to place it on his nightstand.

I put my head between the crook of his neck and I inhale his scent.I don't feel it but soon I feel myself drifting to sleep.

"Good night mi amor" I hear Xander say and kissed my forehead and soon I drifted to sleep while my dear Mate is playing Fortnite while I'm resting on him.

With one last thing being on my mind.

TOMORROWS CHRISTMAS, and yes I put the gifts under his tree and the tree downstairs as well.

....

Hey, did you hate,like or love this chapter?!

I loved it it was funny tomorrow I'm gonna try to update twice.

Don't forgot to keep up with the daily updates .

ANYWAYS IMMA GO START WRITING THE OTHER CHAPTERS SO BYEEEE COOKIES!

Chapter 22/Its Chritmas!

I wake up,run to the washroom closing my eyes and trip obviousl y.Why close my eyes? I mean there's a bunch of presents everywhere and I wanna keep it a surprise.

"Ow" I groan

"Your so stupid sometimes" Xander chuckled picking me up from the floor.

I stick my middle finger up at him and stick my tongue out.

He chuckled And sits me on the counter in the washroom.

"Open up" he says,putting tooth paste on my tooth brush,I open up and he puts the brush and starts brushing my teeth for me while I play with his hair.

"Okay now spit" he says and I spit in the sink and he washes my mouth.

He then starts to watch my face,he changes the bandage on my hand when I cut my finger with a knife by accident,it's not even big it's a small cut but him being him obviously.

He brushes my hair for me.

"Can you make a random cute design?"I ask"yes princess I can" he replies and starts on my hair.

"We're having breakfast in bed after" he says and I reply with an 'ohh yasss'

He finished my hair and I awe at it.

(She has light brown hair if you forgot)

"How do you know how to do this kind of design?!I can't even do that!Im hiring you!Your my new hair stylist but only for me" I say and he laughs.

Oh that laugh,kills me every time.

"Of course your majesty" he says doing the bow thing,royal people do.

I grin and he grabs me by the waist and puts me down.

He holds my hand and walks out of the room. I look around his room and there's presents every where.

To show how much they appreciate the alpha,the pack puts presents for him and the Luna which is me by the way.

So now I wonder if I have this much because this is a whole lot.

I sit down in bed and we wait till the food comes which is like in 20 minutes and my lazy ass gets bored easily so I want something to do.

"I wanna fly" I randomly say and Xander looks up from the book he's reading.

"Then fly" he says and picks me up he lays me on his feet,so my stomach is there and it's like I'm flying.

I giggle and laugh,he acts like he's about to drop me and I scream,I hang on to his leg and he almost lets me go when someone says excuse me.

We look still In the same position,one of the maids called Larissa and a butler named Haris both stand there with food and a smile on their faces.

Xander drops his legs and I scream falling on top of him.

"I hate you" I mutter sitting up on top of him.

"I love you too" he laughs and calls them in.

They place the food on the bed and I say thanks,Xander nods and they leave.

We sit next to each other and start eating.

I look and there's my favourite donuts I take one before Xander eats them before me,he's done that before but I made him buy me more because I love food.

I eat it and he chuckled,he then eats and then stares at me.

"What?" I ask munching the melted cheese,and gulping the orange juice.

"Nothing your just beautiful" he says and kisses my head.

"Thanks I'm blessed what can I say" I say,doing a dramatic hair flip.

"Hell yeah you are" he said and I kissed his cheek. Today we have opening presents,lunch at a restaurant with the fam,ball and then I'm going on a date with Xander.

"What you thinking about" he asks "abut how today is gonna be" I say and he grins " You mean your thinking about our date" he winks and I roll my eyes with a smile on my face.

"Maybe" I said and he coos "just say you are" he whispered huskily in my ear,I turn red and hide my face in my hands.

"Your gonna have so much fun today" he says and I jump on him.

"You mean we're gonna have fun today" I say and he nods chuckling.

We finish eating and I need to go get dressed but I don't wanna see what's in my room,I wanna see when we do it with everyone.

"Zandy,do you have some extra clothes for me in your closet?" I ask and he nods saying a yes and going in his closet.

He goes in and comes bag with clothes.

I take it from him and look at it.

"Oh thank you" I smile and he nods back with a big smile on his face,he wraps his arms around my waist from the back and nuzzles his head in the crook of my neck.

I look at the outfit,he has good taste.

"Thanks" he says,oops did I say that out loud?

"Yes,yes you did" he says and I groan while he laughs.

I wear that with beige heals, Xander does my hair again because it got ruined while we were playing around.

"You look stunning,amazing,cute" he pampered me with compliments and I just stood there grinning like a freak.

So the maids took the food out and now we're going downstairs.

Xander is dressed handsomely,he's wearing some nice dark beige khaki pants and a navy blue button up shirt.

"You look handsome" I say and put my hand on the side of his face,he smiles and kisses me,with love,lust,adoration,and everything he's feeling.

We go downstairs and then we see everyone else,there all dressed nicely,Jay,Parker,Maddie and Veronica come up to us and then obviously Jay is the first to speak.

"Took ya long enough" he said earning a playful glare from Xander and a smirk from me.

Me and the girls try not to laugh.Jay rolls his eyes and pinches his mates hand.

Madeline slaps his hand a way and he gives her a cheeky smile

"OPENING PRESENTS IS FIRST ON MY LIST SO COME ON LETS GO AND OPEN SOME GIFTS CHICAS" Madeline shouts.

"Let's start with the one by the big tree" Xander says and they all nod.

We go to the big tree in the big hallway and all sit down around it,next to each other.

(Imagine a lot more gifts)

"Okay who wants to open gifts first?" Veronica says.

"Me! Me!" Madeline shouts raising her hand and jumping in her spot,Jay looks at her with adoration and love.

"Okay"

"So first I'll open..." she looks around and stares at me "I'll open Ariel's first" she says and looks for the box that says from Ariel,which is me hehe.

She opens it and grins,"no way!! You got me the new Huda beauty palets??!! Omg that shit is expensive!I love it thanks!" She says and blows me a kiss,ya I got her palets,lipgloss and heels she's been wanting,with a bunch of other different outfits and makeup from MAC and All he favourite brands.

She opens the others and says thanks to everyone else.

Veronica got her,perfume,shoes,and fake nails,Parker got her a stuffed animal and chocolates,Xander got her an IPad and a MacBook,and last but not least Jay got her a beautiful necklace with clothes,accessories and a new phone which is the iPhone X she always wanted one instead of iPhone 7 Plus.

Everyone soon went they all got what they wanted the most,this wasn't even what everyone got they still had more up in their room under their tree,it was Xander's turn to open up his presents.

He opened Maddie and Veronica's they got him Jordan's,shirts etc..The boys got him a bunch of expensive perfume,all the same because he uses one specific one and let me tell you it smells delicious.

"Now you open the ones Ariel got for you" Jay smirked,I rolled my eyes laughing.

He opened the first one.

"You actually got me a blanket of us on it together?!!!Thats friking Cute! I love it! I'm changing my other blanket!" He says sounding excited and yes I got him a blanket with us on it,it's the first picture we took with me kissing his cheek closing my eyes and him looking down at me with adoration.

He then opens up the next one which was a necklace I got with both our initials on it,he loved it and kissed me all over my face,I got him a bunch of male products and other stuff that we up in his room.

It's my turn and i open up gifts,Veronica got me some body wash from lush

Madeline got me a huge Louis Vuitton bag I opened it and there was a bunch of new makeup,with brushes.

Jay and Parker got me note books and stationary items

"Open mine! Open mine!" Xander says acting like a 6 year old.

I laugh and start to open his and awe at what he got me,he got me lotions,and body creme.

I hug him so tight I think he almost died,I kiss him so hard and he puts his hands on the side of my face while mine are on his chest.

"Okay love birds enough! Go up to your rooms and open More shit up!" Parker said with enthusiasm laced in his voice.

"Who said you were in charge" Xander said raising his brows smirking,Parker raised his hands in surrender.

....

"Okay close your eyes" Xander said taking me up to my room to see my beautiful Christmas trees and Santa gifts.

"Okay open them" he said and I opened them looking at the sight in front of me with shock of how much presents or gifts or whatever.

Okay so I found out I had a tree In my washroom ,did I know that? No because I use Xander's bathroom or washroom.

So I actually have 3 trees and a half including the one in the big hallway.

So the one next to my bed,yes that's the one I decorated you can praise its looks after.

The one on the side of my room that Xander decorated,that was with a lot of gifts.

And the one in the washroom/bathroom

Yes the bathroom was only filled with pandora,Dior,Louis Vuitton and Versace and Chanel.

"Is this all for me!" I squeal falling on my bed and doing an snow angel but not made of snow you know what I mean?

No? Okay I'll stop.

"Ya it is" he says smirking,why though?

I'm suspicious.

"Why you smirking there buddy boy?" I ask "Nothing Open your presents up,this might take an hour or two,ya we'll still have time to go to dinner tonight and the date is today?" I ask " the date is tomorrow because today we won't have time but then before the date tomorrow we have to pack up for the cruise remember?" He says and I nod remembering.

We sit on the floor next to my bed and I start to open everything up,there's cute clothes,Xander got us matching outfits,he got me a bunch of lotion and perfume a bunch I tell ya!

he goes out for a few minutes and comes back with his hands behind his back,I raise my brows and he puts a DOG in front of me! I squeal and run to it.

"Omg a dog?!"

"Yep"

"Is it a girl or boy?"

"Boy"

"Let's call him....Jasper!"

"Yes!Perfect"

"O ma god thanks" I say kissing his forehead,and the other things I got were just wow!

I put the puppy on my bed and take a pic and post it on the gram. I send a pic to the girls and they put kiddy emojis.

I love Xander.

swoons

So after two hours of opening all my gifts I had clothes,accessories,bags,shoes,candles,perfume,makeup,lingerie etc....

I cleaned all the bags and put everything in its place in my room.

Now it was Xander's turn,we went in his room and sat down,he opened all his presents and it was time to open the things I got him he opened the ones with clothes and shoes then he started opening the watches.

"No! You actually got me my two favourite Armani watches! I was gonna buy them but never mind that thanks princess!" He said and kissed me holding my face in place.

....

So I'm getting ready right now for dinner,I'm in Xander's room he's next to me and we're both gonna be wearing a matching outfit.

"Ugh! Xander would you mind helping me" I said trying to zip he zipper for my skirt.

"What if I say no?" He smirked

"What if I'll not go?" I say smirking bag and he sighed in defeat and zipped it up.

I drag him to the mirror and point.

"Damn who are these hotties" I say and Xander winks.

"Those hotties are us" He said and I laughed,I loved the outfit,it's actually an outfit he bought.

"Instead of a chic restaurant can we go to subway?" I ask,I feel like eating subway.

"You want subway?" He asks and I nod "pleaseeeeee" I say batting my eyelashes and pouting.

"How can I say no to that" he groaned "I'm friking whipped I tell ya" he muttered and I grinned.

Oooh yes you are little patoutie.

"How about I take you to a buffet instead,they'll have everything " he says

"But they don't have subway do they now?" I say wiggling my eyebrows,he groaned again " I'll make you a deal,tomorrow we'll go to subway and today we'll go to a buffet" he says

I mean I'm still getting food and I get to put as much as food as I want without needing to pay all that much,and he said tomorrow and tomorrow is in a couple of hours so.....IM IN!

"Okay" I grin and skip towards his door,he follows behind and we go downstairs.

"WERE GOING TO A BUFFET GIRLS!!" I shout when I see them standing with their mates.

"HELL YAA" they both shout,we then do our happy dancing which is twirling around and doing the floss.

Cringes? Ya we'll stop.

The boys are looking at us trying not to laugh.

"Wait YOU GUYS ARE MATCHING THATS COUPLE GOALS!!!" Madeline squeals and is do a hair flip and wink.

....

Okay so we arrived we bout to meet up with all our parents.

"Over here!" Amanda calls,Amanda is Xander's mom,she was so nice the first time I met her and still is.

We all head and take a seat in front of them,I take a seat next to My Zandy and on the other side is Jay.

"Hey moms and dads" we all say in unison,they all reply with a hi.

"So Xander did you drop the L bomb to her yet?" His mom asked and he smirked," I did that a month and a half ago" he replied and his mom smirks back.

"What?REALLY ARIEL AND YOU DID NOT TELL ME?" My mom shouted,she shook her head and I laughed " I'm afraid your not my daughter anymore" she joked

"I took that to the heart" I say that fake wiping a tear.

We all laughed and chatted until a girl came,a specific girl, the slut of the school,I mean I haven't went to school in a month but still why she here? Nobody knows.

She eyes me while seeing what everyone wants to drink before we all get out of our seats to go get food from the buffet.

"Oh hey Ariel you look good today" she rolls her eyes and I stand up,Maddie and Veronica smirk and stand up walking next to me in front of her.The boys look at us curiously while Xander looks like he's gonna stab her.

"First off bitch,I look good everyday okay?You see this?" I said doing a full on 360 turn and then continued to talk "Scrumptious,Delicious You on the other hand, Dry and tasteless. This,me" I say pointing to myself "I am a snack,a dessert and you on the other hand are Prison food.Okay?Lets be clear on that" I say and then Madeline randomly decides to talk.

(Credits for my bestfriend The1andonly7,yes she let me take her roast from her book because she loves me,let me tell ya I feel honoured If you see this boo I love you)

"Preachhhhh"

I laugh and the slut Bianca leaves.

I look at the table to find everyone with their mouths open,except my mom and dad that is.

"That's right!Keep your mouths hanging this is MY daughter,she just roasted her,we thought her well" my dad says tapping my moms back while she nods.

.....

We're all putting food on our plates,me, Jay and Madeline have three plates.

Call me fat I don't give a shit I love food and I'm still skinny.

Suck on that haters!

I go put them on the table we're we all sitting and I take a seat.

Xander chuckled,"you sure you can eat all that" he asks and I look at him shoving food in my mouth slowly while looking at him,what? I'm doing it like I'm in a movie.

"Yes I'm really sure" I say and continue eating,he then did the worst thing someone could do.

He ate one of my fries.

No one and I mean NO ONE takes my fries.

I glare at him and he smirks taking a bite of it in front of me.

So I do what only I would do,I bit his hand.

He groaned "ow!" He put the part where I put him in his mouth and he made a sad face.

Karmas a bitch.

He's been sucking on his finger for two minutes.Now I feel bad.

Xander's p.o.v:

Silent treatment time let's see how she'll like that I smirk in my head.

"Zandy I'm sowyyy" she says grabbing my finger and kissing it.

I stand up and go outside to see if she follows,I tell the fam I'm coming back.

And to my guess I'm right,she follows me.

"Xander?" She asks furrowing her eyebrows ,I just wanna kiss her so bad right now but I'm refraining myself from doing so.

"Xander?Xander answer me,I'm sorry for biting your finger" she says going in front of me,I try not to swoon and move around her.

I try to give her a hard a glare.

Okay let's make this look real.

"No leave!I legit took one fry!"I scream at her,oh god I hate screaming at her,but this is funny it's because of a fry.

She whimpered and she whispered a sorry.

"DON'T SORRY ME!GO BACK INSIDE" I shouted,trying not to hug her,I turned around away from her and walked then I turn around to see if she's still there and I see her crying wiping her eyes,she's not used to me screaming at her that's probably why she's crying,or she's on her period.

Usually if I'd giver her attitude she'd come at me with a shoe in her hands and dares me to speak again.

I mean I have power over her.

She's full on sobbing right now,nooo my little baby.

I jog to her and embrace her,"Hey don't cry I was only kidding" I say and hug her tightly,I hold her up and she wraps her legs around my waist.She holds onto me still crying a bit and I look at her.

"Baby..come on don't do this to me,I'm sorry how can I make it up to you" I say and kiss her forehead,I wipe a tear using one of my hands because the other one is under her butt holding her.

"Buy me ice cream and gold fish CRAKERSSSS from that store" she smiles lightly pointing to a a small convenient store.

"Okay let's go" I say,but before I put her on my shoulders,she's hanging on to my neck and she's giggling.

I enter the store and go to the snack section,I grab 2 packs of gum and hand it to her,I grab a 2 big goldfish cartons,what I want some too,I then go to the freezer and grab different types of Ben & Jerry's , cookies and creams ,cookie doh,cotton candy,vanilla and birthday cake.

She holds some of the items because I can't hold all of them I'm holding her leg so she won't fall.

In the store there was old people,they were looking at us with awe.

I hand the things to the cashier.

"That's 19,56$" the old cashier says and I hand her a 20$ bill,she's about to hand me the change "keep it" I say and she smiles and hands me the bags.

I then hear light snores,I move my head a little and find Ariel fast asleep.

Typical Ari.

I love this girl.

I chuckled and head inside the restaurant,I see everyone chatting and there eyes land on Ariel who's still on my shoulders.

"Guys,I wanna take her home" I say and take my keys out.

"Ya i think it's getting late" Blaire,Ariel's mom says and Jack Ariel's dad nods,I carefully place her in the passenger seat,I buckle her up and I put the things in the back.

I go in the drivers seat and drive back home,when I arrive I take her out holding the bags,I go upstairs into my room and place her on the bed,I then head in my closet,getting her one of my supreme hoodies.

I take her clothes off and I put the hoodie on her,it's really big in her which makes it cute.

She stirs in her sleep and opens her eyes a bit,"Do you still have our little goldfish and icecream?" She asks and I nod smiling "I put them in the freezer and the goldfish is in my drawer" I say ,I left the gum in my drawer too.

She nods saying an ok and puts her hands up,when she does that it means she wants me to carry her and put her under my covers and cuddle with her,so that's what I do of course but not before changing into my pyjamas,I'm not only gonna wear a boxer because it's winter.

Duh.

I go in next to her and she cuddles with me,I kiss her cheeks and whisper a goodnight and love you,she does the same.

We can't sleep without doing that,like she'd wake up if she forgot to say it.

I close my eyes and fall into deep slumber with my Petite(small) angel.

....

4037 Words? That's a flipping first!

Questions sent to me personally:

Question:'We all know who your bestfriend is,it's The1andonly7,would you trust her with your tacos,fries or any other type of small foods like pizza?'

Chapter 23/ Its a Yacht Trip

A riel's POV

"ARIEL!!!" Xander shouts,and I groan sitting up on the couch.

"WHAT?!" I shout back

"Go get our luggage ready sweetheart,we need to be on the yacht in 2 hours" he says,I swear one of these days I'll end up hurting his precious face with MY GOD DAMN SHOE!

"Haha,ya MY luggage,I'll go prepare MY luggage" I say,sometimes I think I'm honestly his freaking Maid or better yet his slave.

"Aren't you gonna do mine too" he says looking at me with his puppy dog eyes, I give him that I don't think so look.

"Ya ,no buddy boy you can do that yourself" I say and he comes closer,ya come closer so I can slap you hard enough to get you to do your own shit.

What can I say?I'm an independent woman.

No your not you lame shit,right when he asked you out or better yet before he asked you out you depended on your Prince Charming.

Shut up mind!! You're exposing me,I mean I guess I could be useful.

"Fine" I sigh and his face beams "Great!Me and the guys are gonna head to the yacht to organize a couple of things."

"Okay and I'll drive there send me the address me and the girls will be there at 11"

Yes ladies and gentlemen for the first time I woke up early,at 8 am today.

I go in Xander's room and grab clothes that will last him for a week,then grabbed his hair comb and swimming clothes.

I put him shoes and add his tooth brush,everything he needs, I then go do the same.

Soon me and the girls arrive in front of the door.

"Bro,Jay made me put all his shit in his luggage,because his lazy ass couldn't do it." Madeline said.

"Same with Parker I was about to freaking swing at him and I'm guessing Xander did too" Veronica said and I nodded my head.

"When we arrive I'm making them massage our backs" I say and the girls nodded their heads laughing.

We then head out all THREE of us, carrying FOUR luggage each.

I'm driving the Mercedes Xander got me for Christmas.

"Oh shit! My little doggy!" I said running inside the house to get Jasper.

I grab my little fur ball and I put him and hand him to Veronica whose sitting in the back seat,Madeline sitting in the passenger seat.

....

Okay so we arrived and we're getting out of the car,The guys are on the states waving at us.

We go to the trunk and pick the luggage up,no we don't carry them,we go to the porch leave them there and go up the stairs.

"Your turn freakers" Madeline says and they groan and go to the porch carrying the luggage.

The Yacht was indeed beautiful everything was luxurious as predicted.

(Pics right now

(Pics done)

We go inside my bed room preparing to go outside for a tan,we decided to match swimsuits but different colours.

Me in the grey,Madeline in blue and Veronica in red.

We go out and i grab sunscreen,we take a seat on those white chairs.

We go and lay on each one,I sit up needing to put sunscreen.

"XANDER!!!!" I Shout at the top of my lungs,he comes running over to me.

"What who died?!Whats wrong?!" He asked looking around panicked,I roll my eyes in amusement.

"No one died you little shit"

"Then why the hell did you shout like that?" He exclaimed and I show him the sunscreen and grin,he rolled his eyes smiling.

He started rubbing some on my legs,then my stomach,he then did my arms and face.

"Turn around princess" he says and I turn around,he rubs some on my back slowly and then moves to my shoulders.

"Done" he says and I turn back laying on my back.

I grab his arm,pulling him down to me and peck his nose.

"Thanks My Amazing Most heroic Prince Charming " I say adding a curtesy and he grins and pecks my lips.

"Here wear these" he says handing me a small bag.

I open it and there's actually two bags but I didn't see the other one.

There's glasses in them,"Awh thanks" I say and wear the white one.

He bought me glasses,I'm gonna cry nowwww.

I need to be a freaking model bro!

"How do I look?" I ask and wiggle my eyebrows

"Ugly"

"Hideous"

Hoes.

Madeline and veronica say,"thanks guys" I say and they laugh

"Your welcome boo" Roni winks.

"You look stunning mi amor" Zandy says and I do a piece sign and laugh.

......

So it's been 2 hours we've been out here and we decide to go in the pool,the boys join.

"Hey how about we play that game we're we sit on the guys shoulder and we try to push each other off?" Veronica suggests and I nod thinking it's a great idea.

"Yay!" Madeline squeals.

There all on the guys shoulders except for me,"I can't jump all the way on top of your shoulders dumb ass" I say pinching Xander's back and he rolls his eyes.

"Fine,lets make this easier" he says going underwater,I feel him between my legs and then feel myself being lifted.

Now I'm on his shoulders,I hang on to him and then we all go to the middle of the pool.

SPLASHHHH!!!

SPLASHHHH!!!

That's freaking right ladies and gentleman I pushed Veronica and Madeline off.

"Sucks to suck boiiii" I yell when they come up.

"Y'all owe me Snacks and icecream !" I say and then Xander laughs,"Giddy up!" I say and then he drops me.

That's right he drops me.

I go up for air,I then attack him from behind his back but being him and his working out that can't happen.

......

Okay so we all took a shower,and yes me and legit everyone got a tan!!

That's a good thing!

I don't look like Casper the freaking ghost anymore.

Right now I'm sitting down on the couch with everyone else,my legs on Xander and a tray full of snacks on my lap.

We're all watching Rampage,it's a movie with the Rock aka Dwayne Johnson in it and so far I freaking love it!

Xander's eating popcorn,shoving some in my mouth even though I have a bunch of snacks,I open my mouth and he feeds me some.

....

We're all going to our rooms, obviously using three rooms.

Me and Xander go in the washroom,brushing our teeth,"Eye brow plucking time" I smirk at him and groans.

Okay so I've been doing this like right when we met,plucking his eyebrows,mine don't need plucking because mine are naturally in form and shape.

Who cares if that's the same thing.

I usually only fill them in,I drag him to the bed and grab my makeup bag,which has two small other bags inside one for my fake lashes,plucker,etc...and the other for my brushes.

I drag him to my bed sitting with our pyjamas,I sit on his lap facing him and I start plucking.

"Ow"

"Ow"

"Owwww "

I roll my eyes as Xander keeps say ow,soon after I'm done we decided it's time for slumber.

We cuddle up next to eachother and fall into deep sleep.

"Love you" I mumbled

"Love you" he mumbled back.

....

HEYY IM BACK BOIIIS

LOVE YOU GUYS SO FREAKING MUCH!!!

WERE ALMOST AT 2 FREAKING THOUSAND?!!

I might faint.

The description I give to my bestfriend.

You know who you are hoe

Chapter 24/ I win!

A riel's POV

"I think the hell not" I say hitting Xander on the head with the water toy,he tried hitting me.

Key word ' tried' we were all playing in the pool on yacht with a bunch of different water toys,me and Xander playing with one.

(I found the pic but look at their knees bended they don't put them in a real pool,they put them on a freaking water mattress)

He then pushed me off with his hand and the log 'stick',I go up and glare playfully,getting back on the log toy again.

"I win babe,no point in denying it." he says sticking his tongue out and I roll my eyes.

He THINKS he won when he clearly freaking cheated.

"I win babe,no point denying that You CHEATED!!" I exclaimed bobbing my head up and down,he rolled his eyes smirking.

That smirk,it always means something when he smirks like that.

And to my guess I was right,he pushed me off the log toy again,I don't know what their called so don't go telling me what it's actually called cause I like calling it this and ya now you've been proven that crazy exists,only on me though.

I go up and attack him,he falls off into the water.

He goes back up and throws me over his shoulder.

"Help!!Hes gonna attempt murder! Help!" I shout and he slaps my butt.

"Not like I didn't already " he mumbled,and that's my turn to slap him.

He kills rogues and other packs that attack him so of course he's killed before,which is something I don't like but he has no choice but to kill.

"Were gonna take a shower and go chill outside" he says,and I grin.

"got my snacks?" I ask playing with the hem of his shirt,folding it and putting it back down.

Up and down,let's go.

I'm honestly not funny so I should stop trying to impress you guys.

"Yeah I did,and I bought you an iPad so you can watch when your bored" he says and I smile at his actions.

All he does is make me happy,spoil me,he does the smallest of things and they make me swoon.

.....

I finsh taking a shower and I wear my underwear and bra.

I then head inside the closet they have in yacht and pick a pyjama,since it's dark outside and we'll be chilling,it will be chilly out so might as well be comfortable as well.

Chilling and chilly?!!

Did I make a rhyme????!!!!

I go out and put my slippers on,I blow dry my hair and I put it in a messy bun.

I go outside and everyone's already outside,I sit next to Xander and he wraps his arms around me,"here princess" he says handing me the bag with snacks in them.

We all engage in a conversation,it gets too cold to my liking and I shiver,I go inside and grab a blanket,and I head back to my spot.

I cuddle up to Xander and he kisses my forehead,my cheeks are so dead due to sunburn and my face well let's just say it's really tanned.

We were talking about what we should do when we go back home in a couple of days,Xander kept staring at me with a smile.

He intertwined our hands, he then lifted our intertwined hands highed until the top of my hand met his lips. He placed a soft kiss on it, never breaking eye contact with me and I almost shuddered at the intensity.

"My heart stops for a split second when you look at me like that." He whispered softly, inching closer and I furrowed my eyebrows in confusion. My heart beated like a drum against my rib-cage. "Like what?" I whispered, too trapped in his ocean blue eyes. "Like you are looking at me like I'm the only one here." He said, stroking his thumb along my cheek and leaned forward, placing a tender kiss on my forehead. It was soft like silk and His stubble brushed my nose and my heart beat increase at how sexy it was.

I then hear Veronica scream " OH MY GOD!! IS THAT YOUR BEACH HOUSE XANDER??!!"

"Sure is" he chuckles and I turn around to look at the beach house,there's other beach houses surrounding it.

(Imagine it's dark out)

I look around in awe at the luxurious beach house and grin.

"We're staying there?" I ask "Yep that whole place is ours" Xander replied,and grabbed my waist making sure I don't fall over into the water.

"Okay princess sit down" he says and I sit back down,next to the beach house there we're small restaurants,and water stores for buying floaties and other water essentials.

We arrive tomorrow morning,how is that far and we still can see?Its far but you can see it clearly.

I place my head on Xander's shoulder and he wraps his arms around me,holding me close to him he places soft kisses all over my face making me blush and the feeling of joy overwhelms me.

I grab the iPad and take it out from it's box

I place the case he got it with on it and take headphones out.

Every couple doing its own thing,me and Zander decide to watch YouTube Try not to laugh.

I'm pretty sure we failed due to laughing to every single one of the videos.

"That was hilarious!" Xander laughed,his laugh is so cute,it's like he's still a kid,but in a good way,it's like music you'd want to listen to it all day.

"Did you see his face?!" I deadpan and we look at each other and laugh again hysterically.

It's 1 am and I yawn trying to keep my eyes open,Xander notices the little gesture and picks me up.

Due to that everyone follows inside,carrying the things we left.

I couldn't contain the laugh that escaped my mouth when Madeline fell on the floor,she fell asleep on the floor!

Jay picks her up carefully and takes her to their room.

"Goodnight buddy's!" I exclaimed,when I'm really tired I do crazy shit like this.

That's why I prefer sleeping at 12 am exactly because that time I'm half awake and half asleep,that means I'm perfectly fine!

But now..I FEEL DRUGGED!

Xander enters our room and gets me in bed,he too gets in and turns off the lights.

"Goodnight Xander,love you" I say against his chest.

"Goodnight mi amor" he replies and kisses my head.

"Your making me pasta tomorrow" I murmur before I fall into deep slumber.

....

HOOIII?!!!HOW YOU DOINNGGGG!!

No I'm not on drugs,I'm just a so called enthusiastic and fun person,you could say?

Anyways you probably don't care about that,I updated yaaay???

Isn't that great?!!

It sure issss!I'll leave now,but don't forget to tell me,

Did you like this chapter?Was it funny or boring?

FollowVote and comment!

Byeeeee!!

Chapter 25/ beach houses and town

X ander's POV

I wake up,squinting my eyes due to the light and then look at the beauty next to me.

Ariel's arms are sprawled around my torso,her head laying on my shoulder and you can hear her soft snores,her chest rising up and going back down.

I run my fingers through her hair and she opens her eyes a bit,smiling.

"Morning" she whispers

"Morning love" I say and she gets up,sitting next to me.

She leans in wanting a kiss and I grant her that by taking her in a sweet and passionate kiss,she wraps her arms around my neck and I smile against her lips.

We pull back and she rests her forehead on mine,"when do we get off?"she asks rubbing her thumb against my cheek.

"In 30 minutes"I murmur wrapping my arms around her,she smiles and then grins,"Come on let's get changed because when we arrive I'm looking around your beach house and then we're going to the small town." She says and I chuckled.

"Okay princess whatever you say"

She giggles and gets up,"no stay here" I whine grabbing her by her hips.

"Ma boy I need to change" she said in a slang way,I laugh and then groan.

.....

Ariel's POV

I go in the washroom finishing my business and then I go out into the closet,I pick a nice suitable outfit for this day.

With the charm bracelet Xander got me while we were on a date.

It was 170$ from pandora and I just love it.

He gets me so much jewelry and accessories but this is so far my favourite,that's why I always wear it.

.....

We all are like 5 minutes away from going into the beach house when me and the girls smirk.

"Last three there owe us 20 bucks" I scream and means the girls sprint towards the beach house.

Why 20 you ask? I mean it's funnier if you add up the money,it will make all of you run faster and then who knows someone might give you a nice laugh by tripping.

I'm kidding,I'm not that evil.

Maybe I am,who knows?

Me and the girls arrive first,the guys,ya they last.

When Xander and the guys come we open up are palms and smirk.

"Pay up my dudes" I smirk and they groan handing each of us a twenty dollar bill.

20,40,60.

60$ woohoo my whole freaking life allowance.

Okay ya no that's not my whole life allowance,as you already know Xander pampers me with a lot.

No kidding,he gave me like what 20 Amex cards full of money in them.

"Who's rich now,I am" maddie says fanning herself with the 60 bucks she has.

Jay just chuckled at his beyond crazy mate and dragged her inside with her doing goofy faces behind him.

We all enter and Xander takes me to our room.

We place our bags down and we head outside meeting with the others,Okay so me and the girls are officially really hyper due to ....nothing in particular.

"First stop we go to is the mall they have here!Its so big! And they have all our favourite stores,but with more and newer products" Veronica squeals,I start jumping up and down like a lunatic and Maddie twirls giggling .

"Okay what are they on?" Jay asks,and Xander rolls his eyes smiling

"There just excited let them have their moment for today" Xander says,

Yes that's how I want you!

We start skipping on the sidewalk next to each other,it takes a 5 minute walk to get to town.

"One kiss is all it takes,falling in love with me,possibilities" We sang and giggle skipping ahead of the boys,I feel arms wrap around my waist and I feel myself being lifted by Xander.

"Zandy"I giggle and he laugh putting me on top of his shoulders,he starts jogging reaching the big mall.

The others are behind us with the girls on their backs,the boys are next to Xander now and they put us down.

"Which shop first? " Maddie smirks towards us

"Sephora" we smirk back and nod,Sephora was on a right corner,I held onto Xander's hand,and I looked up at him grinning dragging him to the store.

We enter Sephora my hand still intertwined with Xander's and we go into a section where they just got new products,I pick up a small basket,and roam through the aisle.

"What about this one" Xander says picking up a pallet and opening it up.

He hands me it and I look at the colours,"Ooh I like it,oh look one of them has my name" I laugh and point to the second one on the third row,he grins and I add it into the basket.

I pick up more items up,okay makeup is my life,but face is still clear without it because I don't add a lot every single freaking day.

(OKAY OKAY ILL STOP...FOR NOW,THIS WHAT SHE BOUGHT!!"

I needed an extra basket,"You need all that?Princess why do you even wear makeup,I see your face without makeup everyday and you look stunning without it."Xander says and I blush," Do you want me to put everything back" I ask, a bit sad May I add because I've never had these products.

He shakes his head no and smiles,"Your buying them but on one condition" he smiles wider and I grin bobbing my head " what's the condition " I ask ," Your only allowed to wear makeup every other day and just try not to wear it " he says.

"Okay!" I squeal and kiss his cheek,dragging him to the cashier,she finishes scanning them," that will be 345$ please" the cashier says and I nod about to take my Amex card,Xander's hand flies right next to mine with his Amex card and I look at him in confusion,he pays,"Why the hell did you pay?" I ask whisper yell at him behind the guys and girls.

"Because when your with me I pay not you,you pay when I'm not next to you" he says and I roll my eyes while he smirks,holding my Sephora bags.

We enter forever 21 and me and the girls sprint to the back where they have the cutest sweatshirts and clothes.

I pick up a bunch of sweatshirts,in size of medium,it depends honestly,I'm usually a small or medium but usually small,sometimes I take large because it's more baggy and cute.

We grab shorts,jeans,sweats then a bunch of other stuff like jumpers.

We head into other stores like Urban planet, Urban outfitters ,Ardene,rue 21,the body shop,lush,Pink.

Okay last shop we're going in is Victoria secret,we're getting lingerie,underwear's and bras.

The boys are back with us after they gave every bag to one of their butlers they brought with them.

So now their eyes are coming out of their sockets,I grab a bunch of pastel colours,"No baby no,your not only getting these,your man needs to see some red and black" Maddie says taking me to where the red lingerie is.

I look behind to find Xander's hand on covering his mouth,with pink tinted cheeks and he's trying not to smile.

My heartbeat increases and I groan while the girls make me buy loads of lingerie and pairs of bras and underwear.

......

We ate at Taco Bell then realized it was 9 pm so we decided to head home and chill.

Me and Xander get into the room and he closes it.

I go through my bag and pick a pyjama,Xander kisses my shoulder then kisses my lips in a sweet tender kiss.

"I wove you" he says,it gets muffled up because his lips are on my cheek.

"I love you too" I giggle and pick up the pyjama.

Xander matches up with me with Reese sweats,their big so when I go to sleep I'm gonna "steal" one of his grey sweats and hoodie because it gets cold at night.

We head to the living room hand in hand and sit on the couch.

The others soon join,

"Tomorrow will probably be our last day here" Parker says," What?!" Veronica screeches and slams her hands on the couch hand board.

"We just came" she whined

"Still,we just got a call saying the pack is being threatened" Xander says," who would wanna attack the pack for no reason?" I ask

"They want to take over the pack" He said

"Which pack would want to do that"

"Blackmore pack"

....

Heyyyy cookiessss I updateddd!

Yaaaay!!!

I'll try my best to update tomorrow too.

GUESS WHATTT?!!IM MAKING A NEW BOOK YAAAAY,THE CAST WILL BE UPDATED SOON

Anyways see ya

Chapter 26/ Fights and apologies

Ariel's POV

After we arrived back home,Xander's been ignoring me completely,he was too busy with his pack,he's been like this for two weeks and honestly I'm tired of all of it.

I know he has a pack and stuff to take care of but before we went back he said that's the last attack their gonna have and then we can have all the fun we want. The only attacks we got before were by rogues,but now that's over with.

That Blackmore pack just has to ruin everything.

I decide to go talk to Xander,knowing he's probably gonna lash out I take the risk.

Because of him I always have dark circles under my eyes and I lose my appetite each time he screams at me.

Even the guys said that's not normal but they said it's excepted because he's stressed and concerned about his pack,I'm not trying to be greedy I know he has a pack to to take care of but I need to be his First priority,is that being greedy?

I go in his office to find him typing away on his laptop with 3 guys there with him.

"Xander" I call out.

"Not now Ariel" he says,throwing me a death glare.

Now it's my turn to get mad,I growl and he looks back up, " come outside your doorRight now!" I say,the boys in the room leave when he tells them too.

I close the door behind them and Xander strides towards me.

"Why do you keep ignoring me?!Why!!Why don't you talk to me,your always busy with the pack and your always yelling at me and now that's actually bothering me!" I scream,his eyes soften a little,but then they harden.

"Don't raise your voice at me! I have a pack to take care of,it's one of my priorities,you better stop with your tantrums!Get out and stay out I need to work!" He yells,his face turning red.

Tears brim my eyes,"you have no right to yell at me Xander!I didn't do anything wrong!" I yell back.

And then my head flies to the side,I feel a burn on my cheek,he slapped me.

Xander slapped me.

He hit me.

I choke out a sob and realization of what he did dawned upon him,a look of guilt reaches his face and he tries touching me,I start crying so hard and I push his hand away.

"Ariel,I'm S-" I cut him by pushing him a side and running to my room,I lock the door and sob uncomfortably.

I soon get tired of crying and fall asleep.

....

Xander's POV

I stare at my hand shocked of what I did,I was so stressed out and mad,that I put my anger all out on my princess,my love,my everything,I slapped her,I would never want to hurt her intentionally,I love her,and it's all my fault that she's sad and crying.

Two weeks,she tried talking to me but all I was worried about was the pack.

The pack.The pack.The pack.

F the pack,she's supposed to be my number one priority,she is,the pack comes later.

I run my hand through my hair and sudden wave keeps crashing down

Guilt is all I feel,I freaking hit her! I'd kill a person if they touched her but that's what I just did.

I'm going insane, she'll probably hate me,I don't want her to hate me.I would die without her.Shes the most important person I have in my life,my mate,my beautiful mate.

I'm gonna make it up to her if it's the last thing I do,I'll do anything for her to forgive me,all I want to do honestly every day is stay with her,spoil her,make her happy,go out with her.

But I just ruined that chance.

'No you didn't,you fool' jack my wolf says.'You have to show her that your sorry,I feel it,she's hurting' he whimpers,making me whimper as well,I feel it to,it burns and it hurts so much.

I decide to call my little sister for a bit of advice,I know what to do but I wanna make sure it's right.

I hit the call button to her number and wait for her to answer it.

"What's up dawg" she answered,I roll my eyes at her weirdness.

"I need you to come over now! My office hurry!" I say

"But I'm with Andrew,and we're eating icecream" she whined like a little kid.

"Lara just get yourself here,bring Andrew and your icecream too if that's what will make you come" I said.

'More like hissed you physco'

"Okay calm your tits you ratchet looking wannabe,we coming " she said and ended the call with a 'hope you shit out what crawled up your ass'.

Waiting anxiously for them to come,the door barges opens and she strides in licking her ice cream,with Andrew beside her.

How does he handle this girls weird ass self?

"Boy what's that important,that you had to ruin my perfect day for?" She asked,

"It's Ariel" I say

"What's wrong with her,i swear if you hurt her big bro I'm gonna shove you 8 feet under the floor" she said,ya her and Ariel are so close,she loves Ariel so much.

"She's sad and it's all my fault" I say explaining everything that happened.

By the end her face was red,I asked her what do I do.

"what do you do!!Your asking me what do you do! You freaking buy her roses,food,a nice letter and and bunch of shit and then you go apologize and comfort her!You think slapping a girl is okay,wait till I tell mom she's gonna beat the shit out of you with her broom stick!" She yells,Andrew flinched and tried calming her down.

"Okay okay calm yourself! " I say and she glares "Calm myself?!You want me to calm myself,if Andrew did that to me I would have bitch slapped him so hard he'd fly back to Australia and land on his god damn house roof" she yelled and Andrews eyes widened,raising his hands up.

"What the hell do I have to do with this" he says and she glared at him,he rolls his eyes and smiles pecking her cheek.

"You better make her forgive you Xander,I'm not kidding,Ariel is the sweetest girl I know and the fact that you didn't give a shit about her for two god damn weeks is crazy,no wonders she's probably hurting right now,listen just make everything right" she says softly and I nod smiling a bit.

Time to make things right.

......

I went to around the city looking for a bunch of things like,a customized letter,flowers, and a bunch of things Lara told me to get,she helped me a bit,I finish and I drive back home,I go upstairs towards her room and find it locked.

I grab a key I keep with me in case stuff like this happens.

I open it slowly and I close it back when I enter,I see her body sprawled on the bed,I go over and place everything a side and look at her face,my heart ached her cheek was red from where I hit her,thinking about it hurts me.

She has tears dried up on her cheek and she has a bit of dark circles under her eyes.

I shake her gently calling out her name.

"Ariel,princess,wake up love" I say,she makes a whine kind of sound,and opens her eyes a bit getting up.

When she finally opens her eyes,they widened.

"Why are you here,leave me alone" she says and it sounds like she's trying to not cry.Like she's holding it back.

"P-princess I'm so sorry,what I did was so freaking wrong and I'm sorry I'm really sorry,and your my number one priority not the pack and I should've never did that,I love you more then anything princess,i'd never lay a hand on you intentionally,even if I was mad that's just so wrong on many levels,so please forgive me" I say begging,she starts sobbing uncomfortably.

And I feel myself about to break down.

Ariel's POV

You know that feeling when your mad at someone and they make you sad,that moment their there and your crying,your mad at them but you also need them you want them to hold you and you wanna just stay with them forever.

That's how I feel right now.

I sob and Xander opens his arms wanting me to come embrace him and that's what I do,I crush him in a big hug and I sob in his chest.

"I'm so sorry" he whimpers,I try controlling my crying.

He then hands me a a cute envelope.

"Open it later" he says and pulls more stuff.

He sets me down,and gives me beautiful flowers.

I smile,"thank you" I say

"that's not all" he smiles back " I wanna make sure you forgive me,so I got you your favourites" he says.

He then hands me a box and I open it and drool.

"You know not everything is about money and buying me things,you could have just got me a letter" I smile slightly.

"Too bad! Jokes on you! I'm always gonna do shit like this whether you like it or not,the only thing us guys like is seeing our girls happy whether or not it's spoiling you or showering you with kisses." he winks and I giggle.

He always gets me stuff even when I tell him not too,he's always spending on me,I feel like I'm waisting his money.

"No your not wasting my money ,stop saying that I do this because I freaking love you" he says and I nod.

What he got me was a stitch stuffy, vanilla bean frapp my fav,a bouquet of makeup and chocolate stuck to a bag of hot cheetos,a bag with a small teddy bear and a bunch of girly things.

I start reading the letter,

Hey princess,

Don't be mad at me please,I love you and what I did was absolutely wrong and you can call me stupid and dumb and crazy anndddd weird cause you have the absolute right to,you know I love you so much and would never hurt you intentionally because your my princess,no your my queen your my soulmate you half of me! So always know that even if I'm moody sometimes I still love you to the entire universe and back

Love your Prince Charming,

Xander.

I awe and attack him,"Your so cute"

He blushes and I giggle.

.....

"Ariel!Get dressed In something comfy" Xander yells from downstairs.

"Why" I whine just wanting to cuddle with him.

"Do you wanna go to the movies or not" he says appearing at my door smirking.

"Ya!" I squeal and run into my walk in closet,looking for a comfy outfit.

I wear my promise ring and I run up to Xander from behind and jump on his back.

"Come on let's go!" I squeal,he chuckles and kisses my hand that's around his neck.

We enter the car and me and Xander look at eachother smirking knowing what I'm about to do I turn up the radio,I put on dance to this by Troy Sivan ft Ariana Grande.

Young ambitionSay we'll go slow but we never doPremonitionSee me spendin' every night with youOh, yeah, under the kitchen lightsYou still look like dynamiteAnd I wanna end up on youOh, don't need no place to goJust put on the radioYou know what I wanna doWe can just dance to thisDon't take much to start meWe can just dance to thisPush up on my body, yeahYou know we've already seen all of the partiesWe can just dance to thisWe can just, we can justDance to thisDance to thisWe can just dance to this

We sing along and bob are heads up and down

When we arrive I'm about to open my door," Don't open the damn door" Xander says and I look at him raising my hands up in surrender.

He goes to my side and opens my door and I start skipping to the entrance,we enter and go in line to buy the tickets.

"Which movie do you wanna watch" I ask Xander and he smirks

"A Quiet Place" he replies

Oh ma boy you thought.

"Hell to the no no no" I say "we are not watching a scary movie,why do you wanna watch it anyways?" I ask

"So you can jump on me and hold me the whole time" he says and I laugh,I pinch his cheeks stretching them out and

"I'll be doing that anyways" I say and he lets a 'Ow my cheeks!my cheeks!' I let go of his cheeks and kiss them lingering them there for a while and he smiles kissing my nose.

I giggle and he stares at me with adoration.

"You choose then" he says,I think about the choices and choose Jurassic world,Chris Pratt here I come.

"Jurassic world" I say and he nods with an 'okay' smiling.

Let's just drool for a second shall we,because that smile is out of this world.

"Hello what movie tickets would you guys like to purchase today?" The women behind the counter asks with a bored tone rolling her eyes.

"Jurassic world" I reply,I hope she she finds a brain back there.

"That will be 20$" Before I could pull out a 20 dollar bill,Xander beats me to it and gives it to her.

"It's a date on me,you don't pay" he says and I roll my eyes smiling.

I drag him to the snack station,we pick out snacks and drinks,we get a huge ass popcorn.

"Okay I'll the drinks and some snacks and you hold the popcorn and some snacks" I say,grabbing the drinks and some snacks.

"Okay,lets go" he says when he's holding his share.

We go and we show the tickets to the guy sitting in front of the movie door.

We enter," back,back" I squeal and fast walk up the stairs to the back.

He laughs and follows,I choose to sit in the middle seat and Xander next to me,

I put my drink in the cup holder and I click the button placed on the leather seat to raise my feet high.

The movie starts and we watch eating our popcorn.

"Damn Chris you is fine" I mutter.

I look to my side at Xander to find him glaring at me.

"He's not Fine I am" he whispers

"AWHH is my little patootie jelly" I whisper pinching his cheeks.

"No I'm way hotter,right" he says and I nod laughing.

"Of course my little Zandy is hotter,heat the hottest and handsome man alive" I whisper back smiling.

He smiles and kisses me,making my heart beat faster.

I lean back trying to watch the movie when I crave sour patch gummies.

I lean on Xander's side because he has them and try grabbing them so right now half my upper body is on him.

"What do you want princess" he asks " gummies my sour patch gummies" I reply and what he said made all the blood in my body drain.

" I Ate them all" he says shrugging.

I glare at him and sit back in my seat mad that someone ate what MINE,you hear me it's mine!

I huff in my seat," I was only joking my little pwincesss" he says cooing,he hands me the sour patch gummies and I grin.

I open the bag and I stuff some in my mouth.

I lay my head on Xander's shoulder and he holds my hand kissing the top of my head.

"I love you" I whisper and he looks down smiling "I love you too" he says and smile.

....

We finished the movie and headed back home.

"But it was kinda sad,when that one dinosaur was left alone in lava" I say and he chuckled.

"Your adorable" he says,I blush at the compliment and cover my face with my hands.

"Don't you cover your face" he says and picks me up Laying me on the bed.

He places me under the covers and I hide under them,his faces then pops down under the covers too and we start laughing like maniacs.

We start doing random things like hold our breaths and look at eachother trying not to laugh.

We act like idiots together and these moments are the ones you need to cherish the most,spending time together is so important and it actually makes you happy.

We then laugh and he falls on top of me .

We pop our heads from under because we couldn't breath under there and we cuddle.

He runs his fingers through my hair and I hum in delight,snuggling closer if that's possible.

"You smell good" I must against him,he tangled his legs with mine.

"Thanks pwincess" he says and it comes out muffled.

"I love you" I say and hug his torso.

"I wove you too" Okay it came out muffled but that was just the cutest thing ever,he sounds like a little kid and that's just freaking adorable,he's like my big baby.

We soon drift into slumber.

....

YAAAAAAASSSS AN UPDATE ZAYMMMM GIRL??!!!

Okay so I was gonna beat Xander for hurting poor Ari but then he does this pretty cute shit and I can't help but swoon.

'You writing the story you little ratchet looking honkey donkey'

SHUT UP MIND,YOU COME UP WITH THE IDEAS!

Anyways ya did you like it???Love it?? That'd be great if you loved it.

Baiiii see you next time!!!!!!

Chapter 27/ Play fight and grocery store.

A riel's POV

I scream as I hear howls,I run out of my room with Maddie and Roni.

And we scream when a brown wolf with red eyes was running towards us,a black beautiful wolf jumps in front killing it.

I go towards it having this feeling inside me urging me to touch the wolf.

The wolf looks up and I could already tell by it's beauty it's Xander's wolf jack,I've seen his wolf at times but now his wolf looks more built and more just...I have no words because it's beautiful.

I touch Jack,Xander's wolf and he stuffs his face between my neck and growls lowly.

I kiss his nose and smile.

But shriek in fear when I see more wolfs from the window,heading towards the pack house.

Xander then transforms back to his human form and I cover him and pass him a blanket that was on the floor while he's putting his shirt on.

"Run inside this room lock yourself in right now!" He growls and I shake my head no.

"I don't wanna leave you" I say tears forming in my eyes.

"I'll be back I promise"

"No,Xander stop I wanna come" I cry and start sobbing scared of what will happen to him out there.

"Princess,I'll be back it's a last fight remember?" He says and I nod sadly.

He's about to leave when a sob escapes my mouth,and I wipe my tears with my hands forming a small fist.

He then turns around and jogs towards me and hugs me," Hey princess I'm here okay" he says and I try controlling my breathing.

"I love you" I say my arms wrap around his torso and I hug him tightly scared of letting go.

"I love you too,so freaking much" he says and I look up smiling slightly,he pecks my lips and looks down at me.

"When all this is over we can go out all we want and enjoy ourselves and do whatever you want and I have a little something for you after we win,I promise we're gonna win,I'll even take you out to buy you ice cream does that sound good?" He says and I let out a small laugh and nod kissing him one last time.

"Be careful" I say and he looks back," I sure will" he winks and blows me a kiss.

....

It's been 2 hours,two freaking hours of sitting in this dark little room,we have nothing to do,there's only five of us here,Me,Veronica,Madeline,Lara,Mariah and Stella, Mariah is my brothers girlfriend,I freaking love this girl,it's his girlfriend of 2 years and let me tell you she's amazing! And Stella she's Ricky's girlfriend.

"I'm about to freaking piss myself" Stella whisper shouted.

"We all are" Mariah replies.

I was just thinking of the conversation me and Xander had yesterday.

FlashBack

"I'm marking you tomorrow,my wolf just has to" Xander says and I look up at him.

"Are you sure? I mean I'm human will it work?" I ask and he grins at me nodding

"Of course it will and plus it will show the wolf you become when I mate with you" he smirks

Mate as in..oh god.

"I thought you were half vampire too? Will I be a vampire too!?" I squeal and he nods.

I'll have fangs,oh ma lord!!!

"So your mating me tomorrow?" I ask

"If you want me to...my wolf really wants to as much I do but I don't wanna force you" he says and I nod.

"You can mark me" I smile .

End of flashback

So ya today I'll be getting marked,I'm terrified I feel like it's gonna be so painful,it hurts enough a human biting you but my man is a werewolf not to mention also a vampire!!

The door soon opens and me and the girls fake sleep right away.

I feel footsteps coming this way.

"There all asleep" I hear my brother whisper.

"I could already tell my little princess is faking it" Xander says and I try not to laugh and act as serious as I can.

"Yep I can tell my girl is faking too,meaning the others are all faking" Jay says and then me and the girls crack up laughing.

"Your actually alive!" I say throwing myself in Xander's arms.

"I sure am just like I promised" he said and I hug him tightly.

Then my stomach growled,he chuckled and we all decided we should go out and eat.

I drag Xander to my room and sit him on the bed.

"You think I haven't noticed that you were hurt" I say rolling my eyes grabbing the first aid kit.

"I can't outsmart you now can I " he says and I shake my head no,wiping some blood of his hands and putting bandages after.

He suddenly picks me up and I squeal," Before we leave remember I had something to give you" he says and I nod,he sits me down on my bed and turns me around.

I feel something cold being placed around my neck.

"There,perfect!" He exclaims and I look down and gasp at the beautiful necklace placed around me.

"It's so pretty" I say and inspect it more.

"It looks beautiful on you" he smiles and kisses my neck,I blush and look at him.

"When did you even have time to buy this?!" I ask wondering when the actual hell he bought it.

"I bought it before I met you,I wanted to give it to my mate and here you are,I actually just remembered I bought it when I found it in my drawer this morning." He laughs and I peck his lips," well I absolutely love it" I grin and he picks me up spinning me around.

"Glad you do"

....

Right now I'm in my room with the girls we're getting dressed,yep guesses right they got their clothes into my room and now we're all changing together while we gossip,some of you might find it weird but what can I say you probably do it too,if not your friendship is plane normal.

Our friendship is the crazy friendship.

I'm dressed in a cute comfortable outfit that hopefully gets 'accepted' by Xander and isn't qualified as the non outdoor outfit.

I'm wearing the promise ring he gave me a while back.

We all go down and I take my car keys out,

We decide to go girls in one car and boys in another,I'm driving of course and Mariah called shotgun.

"Bitch I'm her bestfriend!"Maddie says sending glares at Mariah and the girls and boys laughs.

"All four of us are her bestfriends!" Roni says rolling her eyes.

"I'm guessing I'm the excluded one?" Lara says rolling her eyes.

"oh my Jesus Christ shut up! All of you!! We're all bestfriends! And Mariah already called shotgun" I exclaimed throwing my hands up in the air.

Suddenly Andrew starts growling and his eyes go black.

"Mine!" He says and pulls Lara to him,she looks stunned and then starts blushing.

"Finally! It was so obvious they were gonna be mates!" Parker said and it's true it was pretty obvious.

Xander and Ricky smile happy for their sister,they hugged her and kissed her forehead.

"Awh does my little Ari want me to hug her too" Jack my idiot of a brother says,coming over and hugging me with a smirk.

"Awh does my little jacky want me to punch him" I say smiling innocently at him.

He just laughs and I join,he kisses my forehead and I kiss his cheek.

.....

"You double decker biscuit!" I say,trying to glare at Maddie from the rear mirror of the car,we'll be at the restaurant in like 10 minutes.

The little girl had pulled my seat back that concludes to me almost hitting Stella in the face with the seat.

"Let's sing!" Lara squeals.

"Rise by Jonas blue and jack and jack!We all sing!" I say and they all reply with a yes!

"We're gonna ri-ri-ri-ri-rise 'til we fallThey said we got no no no no future at allThey wanna ke-ke-keep us down but they can't hold us down anymoreWe're gonna ri-ri-ri-ri-rise 'til we fall" we all start,

"When we hit the bottom, then it goes upClimb to the top with youWe could be the breaks, ones who never made yeahI could be talking to youThey tryna hate hate hateBut we won't change, change anything at allWe're gonna ri-ri-ri-ri-rise 'til we fallThey think we just dropped outLiving at my mom's houseParis must be so proudThey know it allThey don't speak our languageThey say we're too savageNo, no we don't need them anymore

We're gonna ri-ri-ri-ri-rise 'til we fallWe're gonna ri-ri-ri-ri-rise 'til we fallThey don't speak our languageThey say we're too savage, yaNo, no we don't need them anymoreWe're gonna ri-ri-ri-ri-riseWe're gonna ri-ri-ri-ri-riseWe're gonna ri-ri-ri-ri-riseWe're gonna ri-ri-ri-ri-rise 'til we fall

Say we're going no no no no no no nowhereBut we they don't know know know is we don't don't careWe're gonna keepin' on, keepin' on going til' we can't go no moreWe're gonna ri-ri-ri-ri-rise 'til we fall, yeah

When we hit the bottom, then it goes upClimb to the top with youWe could be the breaks, ones who never made yeahI could be talking to youThey tryna hate hate hateBut we won't change, change anything at allWe're gonna ri-ri-ri-ri-rise 'til we fall

They think we just dropped outLiving at our mom's houseParis must be so proud, they know it allNo, hey don't speak our languageThey say we're too savage, yeahNo, no we don't give a- anymore"

We sing and sing and then finish the song,we play 2 more songs and we arrive.

We all get down giggling,right next to us was Xander's car.The boys all get out and look at us," we could hear your singing from our car" Jay says and I roll my eyes.

"Okay first the windows were open and you guys were right in front of us" I say,"You gotta admit we were awesome,we should make a band!!" Lara squeals,shes always bubbly it's a good thing though.

I mean at least she's not depressed.

We enter the restaurant called Liza's and go sit down at a table that well fits twelve people.

"What do you wanna order princess" Xander says while I look at the menu with him.

"I mean is this supposed to be breakfast or like is it brunch " I ask

"Whatever you want as long as your gonna eat it and your happy with it"

"What the hell?! A freaking taco,one only one is 5 dollars" Veronica says her eyes wide.

"So?" Parker replies," we're rich for a reason" Xander shrugs.

"Buy whatever you guys want us guys are paying Okay?!" Xander continues and we all nod with a smile.

We ordered so much,

We had a lot but I was also craving curly fries,so like why not ask Xander to order it for you.

"Xander can I get curly fries" I whisper and he looks at me with a smile," of course you can as I said anything you want,let me guess you want me to ask"he says and I nod.

What? Do you want me to look like a Fatass?

"Get me a curly fries" he says to the waiter in a cold tone.

I glare at him for being so rude and he rolls his eyes a small smile appearing.

The waiter comes back with the curly fries and I take one in my mouth right away.

"Oh god this is so good" Maddie said taking a bite out a chicken wing.

"Everything is good" I say and they nod.

....

Right now I'm in the grocery store with Xander,we're buying things for me of course,you know like icecream? Because we all need ice creams in our lives.

I throw in a bunch of ice creams.

Xander being his extra ass self grabs like what twenty Ben and Jerry's?

Xander rolls the cart and me next to him adds a bunch of noodles,snacks etc...

"I want chips" he says "off to the chips section then" I grin and he speeds with the cart to the chips section.

I start by looking at one chips at a time picking flavours.

Xander,him don't even ask he put them ranch Doritos in,he put ruf-fles,popcorn,hot cheetos etc...

"Ariel can you drag the cart now" he whines,I sigh and let out a huff.

"Fine" I say taking the cart from him.

He adds a bunch of fruits,juice and all those stuffy stuff.

"Boom" I say slowly crashing into the side of his leg.

"Do you want lemonade and fruit punch juice" he asks and I look at him with that 'You already know the answer look'

"Is that even a freaking question?" I deadpan.

"You're paying,you're paying" I sing and he rolls his eyes chuckling.

I see a bunch of teen girls giggling and I look over to them.

They then come up to us,"Hey can we take a picture with you guys?" Little brunette here asked and I smiled.

"Sure" I say and they take a bunch of pictures with all of us.

Then an emo looking girl comes up," I want a picture,but only with him" she says pointing to MY man.

Ya honey..of course not.

"Haha,ya no" I say and Xander smirks rolling the cart forward and I skip towards him linking my arms with his.

"Cupcakes!" I squeal and grab 3 boxes of cupcakes

We arrive at the cashier and I add a pack of gum to the items.

Xander paid and we head out.

....

Right now I'm in Xander's big ass t-shirt and he's in his shorts and t-shirt.

We're on his bed chatting and I'm over here laughing like a dying hyena who's on crack.

And then he suddenly flips me over and that's my friends how we started play fighting.

"Fatass how much do you weigh?!I could turn into a piece of paper with you on me" I say and he rolls his eyes.

"Have you seen these abs" he says lifting his shirt up,okay ya ya he has an 8 pack but what I can't let him know I find them really drool worthy,he'll simply think high of himself.

I try flipping him over and huff out when I can't.

I suddenly go up on top of him and hit him with pillows.

He then does this move and I fake that I'm hurt,let the dramatic effect begin.

"you hurt me!" I say holding my arm,he looks at me with wide eyes and guilt fill his eyes and I mentally high five myself.

"I'm so sorry where does it hurt?" He asks touching my arm.

"It hurts so bad I think I'm gonna die" I say in a high pitch white girl voice and he rolls his eyes knowing I just played him.

I get up laughing and I kiss his cheek,he grins and pouts his lips.

"Who's my little baby you are" I say and he gives me a glare.

I raise my hands up in surrender and laugh.

"I love you" he says and I grin,"I love you too"

"Remember I'm marking you" he says and I grin nodding.

....

HOIII UPDATEDDDDD!!

Rate this chapter?

Any questions for ya girl over here aka me?

Did you like this chapter?

ANYWAYS LOVE YOU BAIIII,UPDATING TOMORROW SO STAY TUNED!!!!

Chapter 28/ Marking and foot massages

"That's 89,56$ please" the cashier says and I hand her a hundred dollar bill and she gives me the change.

I head out into the BMW and go back home.

Confused? Well today is interesting day you can say,why? Well first of all I'm being marked let's just hope I don't pass out ,second of all I'm buying a Xander a couple of gifts,third of all me and the girls will be talking about Valentine's Day and then last but not least me and Xander will be hanging out because I love him and why not?

I arrive home and run upstairs into his room placing the things on the bed.

I call Xander and wait ti'll he comes.

Xander POV

"Xander!" Ariel calls out and run upstairs into my room to where she's coming from . I open the door and my heart drops and a smile spreads at here cuteness,gifts are placed on my bed and I grin.

"What's this?"

"Well a small gift" she shrugs and I hug her kissing her all over her face.

"I love it" I say and my heart beats fast and my face flushed red.

No ones ever done anything like this for me,except her she always finds ways to surprise me.

"When do I get to mark you" I say wanting to mark her so bad.

"Hmm later" she smirks knowing that will torture me.

....

Ariel's POV

"Valentine's Day is literally the best day,well other then Christmas" Lara squeals and me and the girls all nod squealing with her.

"You guys wanna go shopping together tomorrow and find a gift for the guys?" Stella asks and we all reply with a yea.

"It's gonna be lit!" I say and fist bump the air,Xander is gonna mark me after me and the girls finish.

I'm nervous as hell,I don't want it to hurt but he said when he bites in it will hurt just a wincy bit.

After me and the girls finish talking we decided to hang later,with a wink and a good luck from Roni and Maddie,I head into Xander's room to find him placing a bunch of board games on the side with some snacks.

Being real with ya my whole nightstand drawers is filled with snacks.I eat some each day but each day I get more so it's hard to finish them all.

By some I mean like 5 things bags a day,call me crazy if you want.

"Hey what's all this?" I ask and jump on his back.

"Well after I mark you I kinda wanted to have you to myself so I maybe like a home date?" He says his blushing.

"Mark me"I say and his eyes widened.

"Now..?"

"Yeah now when else" I dead pan smiling,he comes towards me and sits me on the bed.

He kneels in front of me and moves my hair away from my neck,I tilt my neck and he rubs the spot he's gonna Mark.

This is a free no inked tattoo.

"Ready princess" he says and I nod squeezing my eyes shut,I feel his fangs in my skin and it hurts in the beginning and still kinda hurts after but you get used to it.

He licks the spot and I smile and run into the washroom and there was a white wolf and a black wolf,knowing the white wolf is mine I awe,I'm a werewolf.

I'm a fudging werewolf,and the vampire is like the bonus cherry on top.

"It's beautiful" Xander says kissing it and I smile,"it is"

My mouth feels suddenly starts burning "Xander my mouth hurts" I say and he just smiles,I'm like dying and he's smiling.

"Your fangs are coming out"honestly I though I'd become a were-wolf/vampire when we mate,but guess not,happens when he bites into me.

I look at my teeth and see the my fangs are out,"Awh baby your like me now" he says and kisses my nose.

"Will it stay like that or does it go back to normal"

"It goes back to Normal,just want you want them out there gonna come out,and for your werewolf,it's gonna come out later when your wolf starts talking to you"

"This is crazy! I'm not sure if this is right,I mean I get to live but I just don't know,what if something ju-" he cuts me off by placing a kiss on my lips and my cheeks heat up.

"Shut up" he smiles and I pout.

"I love you" he says placing his forehead against mine," And I love you"

....

Me and Xander's bond is so freaking strong,like we can't get enough of eachother,well right now he's kinda disappointed that I keep winning,we're playing cards and the game speed but me being me is just too good at that shit.

"I give up!" He says throwing his hands in the air.

"Awh really I'm glad you" I laugh and he glares,he throws a sourpatch gummy bear at my forehead and I tackle him.

He falls back with a thud and I smile sweetly," You do not throw that at me,that is my child my dear precious child" I say and he starts laughing and holds me nodding.

......

Right now Xander is massaging my back while I'm laying on his lap.

"Mhm" I let out enjoying the feeling,he kisses my head and continues.

"Yo big bro" Lara calls coming in from the front door,"What do you want Lara"

"You know it's Valentine's Day soon right"

This girl.

"Yeah I know" he says and smiles down at me,he starts playing with my hair while Lara decides to go back,he stops and takes his hand off and I groan and grab his hand putting it back on my head.

"I love you" I murmur "love you too-" "so much" he says and I smile kissing his thigh.

I then fall into slumber tired.

....

SORRY IF IT WAS BORING NEXT CHAPTER IS INTERESTING I SWEAR,SCHOOL STARTS IN TWO DAYS AND BEEN BUSY!!

But I'm going back to updating almost daily

You know who you are bestfriendddd

Chapter 29/ Girls day

Ariel's POV

"And as I told you before I'm going"

"I said I'm coming" Xander replied rolling his eyes.

"No your not,it's only girls" I reply annoyed with his attitude at the moment.

"It's only girls" he mocked and I glared and he became the most innocent person after I glared.

"Fine" he whined and I smirk in victory and kiss his cheek.

"I love you" he murmured against my hair after showering my face with kisses,"and you know I love you too" I grinned.

I went downstairs and called the girls so we can all match you know cause that's what we're here for?

No okay okay I see you

"What are you a fashion stylist now"Maddie asks and I smirk.

"Yes sisterrrrrr" I say imitating James Charles.

"Okay so what the hell do you wanna match with" Mariah deadpans

I honestly didn't think twice and I pulled out outfits and smirked.

"Damnnnnn girl" Lara says and the girls laugh,I set them on my bed and assign them to wear the ones I got them.

"Ooooh I'm telling you guys are style is amazing no one can relate except for us we're friking uniquely unique" Mariah giggles like a child,sometimes I wonder why were all even friends,gotta love em though.

we all get dressed and we played east side that's my shit right there.

"WHEN I WAS YOUNG I FELL IN LOVE MAN,WE USED TO HOLD HANDS THAT WAS ENOUGH ..." we sang and sounded like we were drowning but who cares? Not us.

We finish up and head downstairs,cause downstairs is where are mans sitting playing Fortnite,is that thing still even famous?

"Babe " I call out,"yeah" he says paying attention to the game.

"I'm gonna leave now"

No answer

"I'm gonna leave"

No answer

"Bih I told you I'm friking leaving!" I say loudly and it caught his attention,he dropped his controller while the other boys are still playing.

I glare at him and he pouts " I'm sorry" he says and pulls me to his chest engulfing me in a hug.

"I love you" he says looking down at me

"Sure you do" I reply

"Hey I'm sorryy" he whined

"I love you too big bear" I say trying not smile at his cuteness,he kisses both my cheeks and pecks my lips.

"Have fun princess" he says and I wave bye

"I will"

......

"Oooh yasss get that you look hot" Lara says telling me buy these five dresses I tried on.

"Would Xander like them" I say eyeing them.

"Of course he will! You look hot!" Madeline says and I give in ending up buying the dresses.

I love Xander so much, I wanna look good for him.

...

We hit a other shops and my legs are killing me due to that.

Well it's mostly Lara and Maddie's fault for making us walk all over the place.

I miss my cookie,as in cookie I mean Xander,it's so weird being away from him.

Me and the girls head out,I'm crossing the road to get to the car ,the last thing I hear before I fall to the ground was, "Call Xander!!"

......

Xander's POV

Me and the boys are playing COD at the moment waiting for the girls to get back,my phone starts ringing and the boys pause the game.

I look at the caller ID and it's Lara,the guys look at me confused and I answer.

"What's up?" I ask

"Xander!?Xander you need to come fast! Oh my god!" She screams panicking

"Lara!Whats wrong!" I stand up

"It's Ariel!S-she got hit with a car! Oh my god please come fast!" Suddenly the world around me stops and I drop my phone to floor and my wolf whimpers.

No,no,no this can't be happening.

....

OMGGGG AAAH I FELT SO BAD WRITING THIS BUT OOOOH TEAAAA

I FINALLY UPDATED?!! YAAAAY

ILL BE UPDATING WAY MORE BEEN BUSY WITH SCHOOL

LOVE YALL PCEEE

Chapter 30/ I need you

X ander's POV

I let my tears fall freely for the first time,I might lose someone who means the world to me.

"We're not loosing her" I tell myself,it's true we're not my babygirl is strong.

I look at her admiring her beauty even when she's laying in a hospital bed she still looks beautiful as ever.

I lay my head on her,sighing it's been 1 week and she's still not awake,my heart sinks and I sob.

I just fell apart,I feel completely helpless like I can't do anything,"Ariel please wake up,please I need you,I-I'm scared of loosing you,you can't leave me babygirl your strong I know you can go through it,I'll give you anything you want,anything just wake up for me please" I say,I feel her hand squeeze mine slightly and I bolt up,I see her squinting her eyes and I smile,so happy,she's awake!

She puts her hand over mine and opens her eyes

"Hi" she says groggily and smiles,"Hey" I whisper rubbing my thumb alongside her cheek.

"How long was I out for" she asks sighing " 1 week"

"What happened again?" She asks and my jaw clenched thinking of what happened.

"A-A car hit you" I reply thinking of the way I killed the guy,turns out the attack was planned,but I sorted everything out and confronted the guy myself.

"Am I gonna die"

"No love your not"I laugh and kiss her," I missed you so so much" I say laying my head on her,"I didn't I saw u eating my food in my dreams every night but I did miss ur face and u" she says and I put a head on my heart fake hurt.

"Wow"

"I'm just kidding you little goof ball" she says and kisses my cheek.

"Do u want anything?Whatever u want name em." I say and she hums thinking.

"Fries,sour jolly rancher drink, my stuffed animal,snacks " she shrugs gulping down the water.

"I gotchu baby girl" I say and stand up," I'll be back okay?" I say and she nods smiling,"kiss before I go?"

"My breath smells disgusting " she says and I shake my head no.

"I don't care,and plus how would it be disgusting if I always rubbed tooth paste on ur teeth" I say knowing she doesn't like missing a day without brushing her teeth,I didn't have toothbrush so I use my fingers while she was in a coma.

"Awhh baby" she says and grabs my hands pulling me down and kisses me.

"I love you"

"I love you too Zandy" she giggles

...

I went to McDonald's and ordered a bucket of fries for 11.99& and I then went getting her favourite stuffed animal that I got her,I got everything she asked for and I placed them in the car.

I arrive back at the hospital carrying what she wants,as I said whatever she wants I get,whether it's foot massages,a nice bath,clothing etc.. anything I'm getting or doing it for her.I spoil this girl,I cherish her,I'll soothe her when she's sad anything only for her.

"Yay your back" she grins and I place the things next to her.

She stuffs fries in her mouth,she's probably so hungry,I'll make her proper food at home,we both eat together since I barley ate the whole week.

I got two of the same drinks because I knew we were gonna devour em.

"Hey Babe" She says and I look up

"Yeah princess?"

"Can we cuddle" she asks

"I don't wanna hurt you"

"You won't please" She says giving me her puppy dog eyes.

"Fine" i say as I move everything and grab her stuffed animal,she moves over and I lay next to her,cuddling.

......

Ariel's POV

I'm honestly the luckiest girl,Xander takes care of me so well.Hes the best thing that's ever happened to me.

We cuddle as he plays with my hair,I sigh in content,"Want a bath when we get home" he asks and I nod,feeling the need to getting washed.

We arrive home and he carries me to the bathroom inside my room,he sets me on the counter,I take my clothes off and he starts the water,grabbing a towel and setting it next to the bath.

He grabs a bath bomb and sets me in with it,the bubbles starting.

"Can u come in with me" I pout and he laughs," of course " he says and gets in splashing with water.

"Hey" I laugh and he smiles pinching my cheeks.

"I love you so muchhhh " He says peppering me with kisses.

He was my life............

HOPE YOU LIKED THE CHAPTER!!!

Chapter 31/6 kids and the carnival

A riel's POV

"Gimme that no no no" Jay sings,those aren't even song lyrics what is this guy singing.

"Ooooh no no no" Parker continues doing random moves.

"Can you guys stop you guys look so weird and is that even a song babe?" Madeline says munching on the Oreos she bought.Stella,Lara and Mariah are watching Netflix on the TV,My brother,Ricky and Andrew are playing COD in my brothers room,and Xander?

He's still sleeping like a baby,I'm honestly bored without him,I wanna go wake him up but,ya no but I'm going.

I go up to our room,and there he is sleeping like no tomorrow,I smile at hoe lucky I am to have him,I wouldn't trade him for the world I just love him,everything about him,his scent,the way he talks to me and the way he treats me,he's everything a girl can want.

A couple strands of hair fall on his forehead,his hair isn't short and isn't long it's perfect for me to play with or to just grab it,it's so soft.

I go and kiss his cheek down to his jaw,his eyes flutter open and he smiles.

"Hey beautiful" he says groggily due to him just waking up,can a women just faint,he's the most adorable human being ever.

"Hey baby" I whisper,trying to hug him but it's kinda hard due to our positions.

He chuckles and pulls me up making me straddle his waist.Kissing his jaw and then kissing his lips.He kisses back wrapping his arms around me,our lips moving in sync.

We break apart and I kiss him again,I swear it's like an addiction.

"Baby are you okay?You won't stop kissing me" he laughs and continues" I mean I'm not complaining"

"I-I I'm addicted" I say and lay on top of him,"See I am addictive,most I say it's the looks" he smirks and I laugh. He kisses both my cheeks and then kisses my nose,then my forehead.

"Gosh I love you so much" he says stuffing his face between my neck,playing with my hair.

"I made you food" I grinned and I get up,"Really?" He asks and I nod.

I made breakfast for him knowing he'd be hungry.

I go downstairs and bring it up to our room,it's all on a tray and to make it cute I added a small menu.

"Oh lord the goddess blessed me with you" he says and I place the tray on his lap.

"A menu? Waffles,Eggs,strawberries,kiwis,and Nutella" he says reading the smallMenu.

"Isn't it cute" I smirk and he nods,"But it'sMissing something" he says and I look at him in confusion.

What am I missing,is he not satisfied I literally burnt my hand doing those damn eggs.

"What's it missing"

"You" I just stare at him shocked,my mouth falls open and I close it back.

I am shook.

"Damn" I mutter and he laughs holding his stomach,"you should've seen the look on your face" he laughs and I glare at him playfully rolling my eyes.

"These taste so good" he says closing his eyes,I smile happy of my work.

After he finished eating we decided to go out for a walk,so I went in our closet and picked out a comfortable outfit.

I get out and Xander is wearing a grey hoodie with black sweats,and a Nike hat,he looked extremely good with his hair slicked back and his muscles showing.

"Come on now princess" he says putting his hand out,I take a hold of his hand locking our fingers together and we head outside.

We start walking comfortably,"Wanna get food later?" He asks and I nod,"McDonald's" I grin " Perfect"

"I want 2 kids" I say out of nowhere,he looks down at me surprised then he smirks,"No"

"What why not"I whine,"Because I want a whole basketball team,or even more" he says and I look at him my eyes almost popping out.

"Ya why not adopt the whole country next" I reply sarcastically,he huffs and sticks his tongue out looking like a cute baby.

"Okay fine at least 6?" He says,I think about it and give in.

"Fine 6 max" I say and he grins,"That's after I put a ring on that finger" he whispers in my ear,making my face go beat red.

"Yes" I say,"huh" he says confused,"I accept your marriage proposal from now " I say and he burst out laughing,attracting attention.

"Now I don't need to be afraid of your answer when I actually do get on one knee" he says and I smile,giggling.

Out nowhere he stops in front of me making me hit his back.

"Ow!What the heck Xander! I think I broke my nose thanks to you stopping out of no where" I say rubbing my nose and he looks down at me,he laughs,he freaking laughs at me.

No he doesn't help and ask if I'm okay like any other mate he freaking laughs.

"Guess what Jackass no kisses for a damn week" I say and continue walking alone,he jogs next to me.

"No" he growls,"Yes" I say trying to make a growling noise like him,but I can't you know why?!

BECAUSE NOT EVERY HUMAN IS MATED TO A WEREWOLF.

"Hey it's not even fair the only reason I stopped was to look at the poster that said Carnival but I guess you don't wanna go" he says and I know for a fact he's smirking down at me.

"Who said I didn't " I mutter huffing out," We'll go under one condition " he says and I nod rapidly wanting to really go to the carnival.

"You kiss me" I obviously wanna go so I give in and kiss him.

"What time do we go?" I ask and he checks the time on his phone," After we eat,we can head back home if you want to change then we can go because it opens up at 7:00 pm"

"Okay sounds good" I smile and re hold his hand.

While walking we spot the McDonald's so we go and head in.

"Food! Finally!" I let out happy we found my home place.

"Hey welcome what can I get you" a girl says looking at her long pink nails looking bored.

I roll my eyes at her rudeness,"I'd like two fish burgers,fries and two cokes" Xander growls,hating the disrespect he's getting.

She looks up and fixes her self, Ah so she looks at my mate but not me her own Luna,Okay that's fine cause I'm not gonna rip her fake extensions out of her damn head.

"Can I get you anything else Alpha" she purrs,what is she a freaking cat now?!Xander looks extremely disgusted.

I've been trying to compose myself but I need to lash at this full on plastic Barbie to let her know who she's dealing with.

"Do you not see me or are you blind?" I say furiously,"And You are?" She says,"You'll know who the hell I am when I rip your eyes out" I threatened.

"She's your Luna" Xander booms "And in your Alpha and you will be punished for behaving in a non tolerated way"

"Yes Alpha I'm sorry ,sorry Luna " she says bowing her head.

"Better be" I say flipping my hair being dramatic and walking to a booth.

Xander following me earning bows from everyone.

"Babe sometimes you scare me when your hungry " he says and I shrug,"What Can I say I'm a badass,I have this aura " I laugh and he smirks," My badass" he says and I giggle.

The food soon arrives at our table and I'm glad because I'm Hangry.

"Feed me a fry" he says and I look at him weirdly,I feed him it.

"Can't you feed yourself?" I ask biting into my fish burger.

"It taste better when you feed me"

"Your gonna be the death of me"

....

So we arrived home and right now I wanna change because why not.Xan der didn't wanna change so I let him be.

We head out and we decide to go in his Mercedes Benz,I run to it and open the door when I hear a growl.

"Okay big wolf I'm not gonna touch it" I say putting my hands up in surrender.

.....

We arrive at the carnival and Xander pays for the tickets okay the last time I used my Card was like 3 months ago he literally never lets me pay or else he'll be sad or mad.

We head in and I look at everything in Awe."What do you wanna do first?" He asks and I look around,I jump up and down and point to the game section," I want to win a bear even though I already have the ones you got me I want another one" I laugh and he chuckles I drag him there and he starts to play it.

"Yay!" I grin when he wins,I hug the bear and peck his lips then I skip towards a girl who's Selina gold fish,"Can we please get a fish!I promise I'll take care of it!" I pout giving him my puppy dog eyes.

"Fine" he says and we go get a gold fish,I then go and play a game which consists of me throwing rings and hitting the highest score which gives me a balloon like floating guitar.

We play other games which earns me winning more stuffies.

Someone then comes and asks if we want a photo so me being me said yes and asked Xander to do a fish face.

(Not them but how the picture was took)

"Lets go on the roller costed moving thingy" He says and I smile wide and we hop on.

It's a Ferris wheel stupid.

"I-I'm scared of heights" I say trying not to look down,"I'm here don't worry your fine love" he says hugging me close to him,while we enjoy the night sky and all the neon lights.

He kissed me and I kissed back savouring every moment.

Soon the ride ends and we hop out,we head back in the car and head home,when we get there we get dressed in pyjamas and I put my fish who's name I called Nemo in a cute fish tank.

We go under the covers and Xander turns the lights off.

Wrapping his arms around my waist he pulls me closer and kisses my nose.

"Goodnight my Juliette"

"Goodnight my Romeo"

....

Heyyyy there the second update!

I hope you like these fast updates

Love you -Zeinab Bazzi

Chapter 32/Heat and mood swings

Ariel's POV

"I will hurt you" I glare at Xander,he's being so annoying right now he won't make me food,and he knows what pain I'm going through.

"Why can't I just buy you food?" He whines,"because I like your cooking" I shrug and flop on the couch,someone was definitely sitting here considering how warm the freaking couch is.

"How about I cook dinner,and I'll just order food right now" he tries to negotiate but me being me at the moment has to give out a speech.

"Oh okay,fine by me considering how much you LOVE me you know I'll just ask one of the other guys,better yet since your uselessness isn't helping me at the moment" I bark and smirk in satisfaction when I see how scared he is.

He runs off into the kitchen,"Crazy women!" I laugh silently and sit down putting on Shadow Hunters watching the new episodes.

"Your food is ready!"

I skip towards the table and my mouth waters,"Have I ever told you how much I love you" I say earning an eye roll from him,"Yeah actually after every time I'm threatened! To do your food" he exclaims and pouts,I get off the chair and walk up to him kissing his pouted lips.I eat the food so happy now,he fed the beast.

"Loser" he mutters and I giggle.

"Okay so can we go to target" I say and he looks at me,"Snacks" he smirks and I smirk back,"Oh you know me so well"

"Last one up is a rotten egg" He says and he sprints upstairs I chase after him and jump on his back,"that's not fair" he whined,"too bad my g" I say hanging onto him for my dear life,honestly i could really care less right now,dont blame me,im on my period do you know what a girl goes through?The cramps,mood swings,the extreme hunger and need of attention.

"Get in the room"he says taking me down and putting me on my feet,i huff and walk over to the closet,picking out a comfy outfit i wont die in.Xander chose his and stalked over me checking me out while hes at it.

"I need a couple of things too from Walmart " he says and I quirk an eyebrow,"And then we get more food"I shrug,"Your already hungry?" He says and I shake my head no,"Well I'm gonna be".

He laughs and grabs my hand,"Wait let me get my purse" I say and run to get my purse from Givenchy,Xander bought me on my birthday.

I go and hold his hand again,his hand is so warm and big,I cuddle up to his side while we're walking to the car.

He opens the car door and I head in,he goes to his side and slides in putting the keys and starting the car.I put on Invisible by Anna Clendening.

"What is this depressing shit?" Xander asks and I stare at him,"Depressing?Are you high?How is this depressing?" I say,no my mate does not smoke,drink or does drugs.

"Happy ever after?I don't think soI'm in love with someone who doesn't know I exist." He mocks the song and I roll my eyes,"Fine change it" I say and he puts on DJ turn it up by Yellow Claw.

He bobs his head to the beat,and I smile,he's so freaking cute I can't.

......

We're inside target and I get the cart,"Which aisle first princess?" Xander,"snacks,duh" I say and drag the cart him following next to me,I go and look at the racks looking at the type of candy,chocolates and chips.

"I want all of them but I can't have all of them" I say debating on which ones to get,"Who said you can't get all of them?Get everything you like princess no ones stopping you" Xander says and my eyes widen then I bounce up and down.

"Really?!!" I giggle and he nods,I skip and grab what I want,Xander picks up as much as me and puts them in the cart,we then head to the Clothes section,they have pretty comfortable clothes not gonna lie they're pretty comfy.

I grab different assortments of Pyjamas for us both and I grab socks,adding them to the cart.

We walk until my ankle twists over nothing,I rebalance my self and Cander hunches over laughing his ass off,"Oh my god,I can't that was hilarious" he says and I roll my eyes walking with the strolley,going to the cash register.

.....

We were at Walmart right now,we finished purchasing things for the house, we went in the car when i felt a burning sensation in me,i let out a cry and hunch over,Xander smells the air and stiffens,and his eyes show lust.

I look at him confused and hunch over letting another cry,"Heat,your in your heat,we have to get you home fast before any other male smells you" he grits out and speeds home.

We arrive and he opens the door,Jay and Parker stand there,and sniff the air,their eyes darkening.

"Jay I swear to god,you will become mateless if you try anything" Madeline says and I wince.

He takes me upstairs and holds me tight,the pain soothes abit.

"What do I do to make it stop" I sob and he hugs me.

"We have to mate" he says his eyes darkening.

.....Sorry for the late update! I love you guys so much I'll be updating again soon so stay tuned babes

Hope you liked this chapter!!

No hate please,it gets good

Don't forget to vote,comment and follow,I mean I deserve it if I'm entertaining y'all

-Zeinab Bazzi

Chapter 33/ Heat

Ariel's POV

"What? As in, make love?" I gulped and wiped my hand across my forehead to get rid of excess sweat.

The fact that I don't get to pick the moment when Xander and I are feeling like we should have sex but instead it has to be tonight unless I want to be in writhing pain.

The word heat was not at all the best way to describe it. My body was on fire and it only seemed to get worse with every passing minute.

"Xander!" I screamed. I needed to feel his touch, to know I wasn't alone in this intense moment of fieriness.

"The bath is almost ready, love!" He screamed back anxiously, trying to ease the pain without him falling into the obvious best way to get rid of this faltering torture.

Xander came running into the room and started to undress me for the bath. I let him do most of the work. He picked me up and dipped me in the tub. I felt the coolness of the freezing cold ice bath. I pick up an ice cube and watch as it melts in my hand almost instantly. I feel normal for about a minute until it starts to get warmer and warmer by the second.

"Does it ever pass," I asked through gritted teeth.

I looked at Xander. His face had no hope yet his eyes were clouded with lust. This was putting a strain on him too.

After all the ice melted Xander ran out for more so I began to refill the bath with cold water. I had my back turned to the door when I heard it squeak open.

"Hey, Xander, can you get some ice cream? The one that's been in the back of the freezer forever and has frostbite of its own."

When he didn't answer I looked back except that it wasn't Xander standing in the bathroom doorway. I didn't know who he was but I knew the look in his eyes wasn't good. He seemed to be restraining himself all the while trying to jump my bones.

I froze and for the first time all day I felt cold.

I wanted to scream but my mouth wouldn't move.

The mysterious man took a step closer and that's all it took for me to break my stone stance and yell.

"Xander!" I began backing up with every step the man took closer. I heard thundering footsteps from outside of the room. Xander was coming but the man wasn't leaving.

I was afraid Xan wouldn't make it in time.

As the man began leaning over the tub which was greater in size compared to most bathtubs I swear time froze and the next thing I knew the man was being thrown through the wall. I felt Xander lift me up in his arms and wrap a towel around me. The towel seemed to be the opposite of a heated one. It felt good against my burning skin.

"I'm so sorry, Ariel. I shouldn't have left you alone." He laid in bed with me while I dried off.

I stared into his eyes and I don't know if it was the heat or just that I loved him but I knew that I wanted him and only him in this very moment.

"Xander , I can't handle it anymore let's get it over with"

"Are you sure!?" He says rubbing the back of his neck.

I bit my lip. I knew I wanted him from the start but this heat has only enhanced my feelings.

I smile and nod. It was all it took for him to smash his lips.

The next morning I woke up exuberant.

It was like a scene from the movies. I woke up with pillow feathers every-where, a smile on my face as I stared at Xander still asleep. I raised my hand to pick a feather out of his hair. Last night was amazing.

I felt so happy I decided to get up and make us some breakfast.

I threw on some leggings and an oversized sweater then walked to the kitchen with a smile on my face.

I told Alexa to play my favorite playlist and got to work.

I was singing to Easier by 5sos when a pair of arms wrapped around my waist. I grinned when Xander kissed my neck and started whispering in my ear.

"You feeling better already," he asked in a naughty connotation.

"Well, of course, you made sure of that." I served the plates and turned around pushing him away to set the plates on the table.

"Bon Appetit." I smiled at Xander feeling euphoric.

After we ate I got ready in a body tight blue long sleeve turtle neck, a black and white plaid skirt, and black heel shin boots. I curled my hair and put on my two James Avery rings. I grabbed my bag and phone then walked out of the house to the car to Xander who was waiting patiently in a black Mercedez G-wagon.

We drove to Starbucks for a little coffee then to the mall. Yeah, I wanted to get some lingerie.

In short, we got shit done. Like the bomb ass couple we are. Truly, a power couple.

We went into Victoria secret and I picked out a bunch.

That wasn't even the first half,we bought other things and went heading home.

....

Chapter 34/ prank wars and mukbangs

A riel's POV

" Alexander Jackson king!! If you don't get your ass here right now I swear to god, your pretty face won't be so pretty!" I scream running downstairs.

I look around glaring, looking for him, I'm beyond pissed. Oh, why?! Maybe because he fucking threw worms at me, as a "prank".

How the fuck is that even a prank ?!

You best believe I'm gonna make him pay.

"Aaaaah" he screams running from under the living room table and into the kitchen, the guys snicker running behind him.

I call Madeline and Veronica and they come running down.

"Who's bitch ass are we killing today ?!" Veronica says bouncing up and down.

" The three little pigs," I said smirking and grabbing Xander's phone that I found laying on the couch, let's just spam his phone a little.

I spammed his phone with pictures of me obviously and some of my feet cause my feet looking pretty cute. Let's hope he doesn't have a foot fetish after he sees these.

I keep his phone in my pocket and Madeline calls me, " we gotta sneak attack, do it the ninja way, the invisible way" she grins and I nod letting out a chuckle. We go on our knees and crawl to the kitchen.

" Shhh you need to calm down, you're being too loud" I hear Jay sing, if you don't know this song, I'm sorry but I'm disowning you myself.

Right now I'm wearing my pyjamas, I was just minding my business until he threw the worms in the morning obviously.

We try not to giggle and grab some flour and put it in a pot with some water. It's no fun without the water. I, Madeline are both holding a pot each while Veronica holds garlic dip.

God knows what she's gonna do with that.

We find them behind a table, where there's a bunch of different varieties of snacks, I could use some of those later. I mean not use, most likely devour.

I smirk and grab a handful of the wet flour and throw it on Xander's perfect hair.

We let out a squeal and throw the rest on them," what the fuck baby!" He whines and tries taking the flour out.

Serves him right.

"I'm hungry now" I pout, feeling totally hungry and just wanting food is really all I want right now.

"Okay let's go get food" he smiles and gets up." Let me shower first" he says and I nod giggling.

"Let me go you fucking beast" I hear Madeline yell at Jay. He pouts and walks off with her.

Veronica looks at Parker and runs, he chases after her and flings her over his shoulder.

"Awh Man" she whines and then giggles after he kisses her cheek.

I just stare at Xander, flip my hair and walk to the fridge.

"No apologies?" He says and I turn around slowly looking at him.

"No " I grin and take out some leftover pizza, I put it inside the microwave and wait.

He comes next to me and I look him up and down, what a sight.

He's covered in slimy flour. So cute.

"Don't even talk to me" he says and I laugh, well someone's butthurt now. "Are you pressed or are you mad, are you upset or are you sad-" I sing and twirl around leaving the kitchen him following after me.

I made sure, we went to grab food because a girl is hungry and me being hungry is not such a pretty sight. Is it just me or do I just eat anything, except for a couple of things obviously cause somethings just taste horrible id rather barf 20 times then swallow it.

Okay, that was really exaggerated.

We went to TacoBell, that place is blessed, don't even argue me about it.

We don't even sit inside, we back and sit in our car.

" Hi" He says and grins, "Hi" I giggle. We start eating and having small talk.

An idea pops in my head and I smirk, I grab Xander's phone and place it on the dashboard facing us.

He looks at me weirdly, " What are you doing?" "Doing a Muckbang?" I say and turn the camera on to his iPhone 11 pro, surely this was definitely good quality although I feel like it works the same as every other phone but we move.

"What's a Muckbang?" He asks confused, I look at him with an 'are-you-dead-ass-serious'

"It's basically when people eat in front of the camera and just talk." I shrug and he nods clapping his hands like a little kid.

"Let's do it!" He grins and I start the video.

"Hey to our non-existing subscribers, I and Ariel are gonna be eating in front of you guys." He says rather calmly and I slap my forehead trying not to laugh.

"Am I not doing it right?" He pouts and I pinch his cheeks, " You're doing perfectly fine, baby." I smile and hug him trying not to smush the food.

We talk and laugh loudly, then I start choking on the food.

That's what YouTubers don't show, 'behind the scenes dying'.

"Are you done?" He asks and I nod stopping the 15-minute video of us basically laughing like maniacs.

....